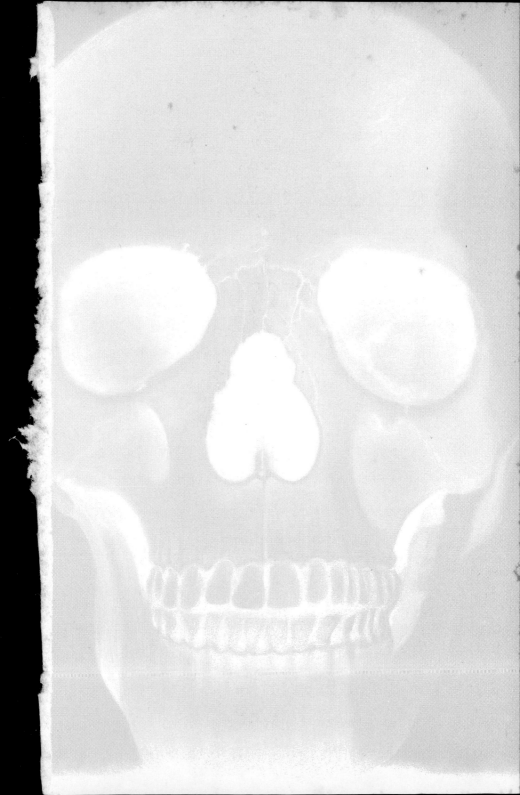

HAMLET

a novel

JOHN MARSDEN

TEXT PUBLISHING MELBOURNE AUSTRALIA

The paper used in this book is manufactured only
from wood grown in sustainable regrowth forests.

The Text Publishing Company
Swann House
22 William St
Melbourne Victoria 3000
Australia
www.textpublishing.com.au

First published 2008 by The Text Publishing Company

Typeset by J&M Typesetters
Printed and bound by Griffin Press
Design by Susan Miller
Cover design by WH Chong

National Library of Australia Cataloguing-in-Publication data:

Marsden, John, 1950-
Hamlet : a novel / John Marsden.
Melbourne : The Text Publishing Company, 2008.
ISBN: 9781921351471 (hbk.)
A823.3

TO WARWICK GREGORY

IN MEMORIAM

O N E

'Do you believe in ghosts?' Horatio asked him.

He was lying on Hamlet's bed.

Hamlet was sitting on the stone floor, in a corner, the corner furthest from the door. The prince was eating strawberries. He smiled. It was the first time Horatio had seen him smile since the funeral. Hamlet traced a line on the stone with his finger. He looked down, watching the invisible line. 'I don't believe in floors,' he said. 'I don't believe in lines.'

'But do you believe in ghosts?'

'I don't believe in walls or ceilings. Or stone. I don't believe in people. I don't believe in strawberries.'

'But ghosts?'

'I don't believe in anything you can see or touch or taste.'

'So you do believe in ghosts?'

Hamlet smiled again. He wriggled, on the hard floor. His eyes, his grey eyes, lifted and met Horatio's. 'My bum's getting sore. Let's play football.'

T W O

They played one-on-one for a while, on a vast grassy area across the river. Towards the trees the frost remained from the night before, cold and hard and beautiful. Soon a couple of officers' sons drifted towards them, looking hopeful. Hamlet invited them to join the game, and full of thanks they rushed in. At first they were too nervous of Hamlet to mark him closely, or to tackle him, but gradually they forgot that they were playing with the crown prince of Denmark and the little match started to flow.

Afterwards, on their way back to Elsinore, Hamlet and Horatio stopped near the footbridge to look down into the river. The water, swollen by the heavy rain and melted snow of a false spring, rushed past. It had the grey-green-fawn colour of a giant snake. Hamlet stared down the steep bank, wondering how it would be to lose his footing, to fall into the fatal flow and be carried to the ocean.

He threw in a piece of bark and followed it with his eyes as it swirled away. Horatio laughed. 'Watch this,' Hamlet said. He flicked a flat stone across the water. It skipped three times then sank violently.

Horatio picked up the football. The boys crossed the bridge. Every few steps Hamlet spat into the torrent, watching the pitiful sparrow of his spit lose itself in the spume.

They swung right and walked up the hill towards the castle. Elsinore dominated everything. The shadow of the great grey wall came down the slope to meet them. Hamlet's white hair stood out like a splash of snow. A swallow flew out of the shadow, swerving as it saw the two boys. To their left, the cemetery, stretching away towards the lake, looked bleaker than ever.

Hamlet hugged himself against the fierce cold. Horatio nodded at the white picket fence, the endless rows of crosses. An occasional headstone or small mausoleum was the only interruption to the monotony.

The gentle slope of the ground made it difficult to see where the land ended and the distant water began.

Horatio squeezed the football with both hands. 'Have you been back here?' he asked. He looked away nervously, though, as soon as he said it. How would Hamlet react? At the best of times it was difficult to reach the prince's heart, to find his feelings, and this was not the best of times.

Yet Hamlet answered easily enough. 'No, I haven't been back.'

Horatio cleared his throat. 'I'm sorry I couldn't be here for the funeral.'

'You made it to the wedding.'

'It wasn't long…' Horatio didn't finish the sentence. Hamlet glanced at him, then gave a grimace that could have been another smile. Horatio was used to the expression; he remembered it from when they played football on Saturday afternoons. They had never won a game.

'It wasn't long between the funeral and the wedding, is that what you were going to say?'

'Well, I guess if your mother is, you know, happy… I mean, it's good that she's got someone…' Horatio, red-faced, cursed himself for starting this conversation. The boys moved a little further along the path, towards the small open gate in the side fence. Tucking the football under his arm, Horatio bounced the flat of his hand on the top of each picket.

'Oh, she had a good reason for getting married again so quickly,' Hamlet said.

'She did?'

'Yeah. Oh definitely. It was to save money.'

Horatio stopped in his tracks and stared at Hamlet. His friend had startled him again. 'To…to save money?'

'Yeah. See, she recycled the flowers. Grabbed them off the grave the day after the funeral and carried them up the aisle for the wedding.'

Horatio laughed uneasily. As usual he could not think of the right thing to say, so he went back to facts, to mathematics. 'How long after the funeral did she get married?'

'Two months. Two months, six days…plus, say, two and a half hours.'

'I guess that is pretty quick.'

'She would have used the leftover sandwiches, but they were drying out a bit.'

'Those flowers must have been tougher.'

Swerving, Hamlet avoided the gate and led the way towards the northern end of the cemetery. He called back over his shoulder: 'Do you ever go and visit your mother?'

'No.'

'I don't visit my father. Anyway they're going to move him soon. They're building that enormous sarcophagus thing over there. But I don't think people are in their coffins. They escape before the lid's screwed down.'

The two boys stopped short of the foreigners' section and leaned on the fence. They gazed at the first row of headstones. The branches of a black tree cavorted in the wind. In this direction the outlook was painfully flat by Horatio's standards; he had to glance back over his shoulder, at the mountains in the distance. His family came from the hills.

When he looked at the graveyard again a man with a shovel on his shoulder was walking down the gravel path, past a row of fresh mounds. Perhaps he buried my mother, Horatio wondered. He looks so old. Would he have been too deaf to hear her fingers scratching on the lid? His nightmare was that his mother might have been alive when she was buried. He liked Hamlet's idea that people escaped from their coffins.

He paused opposite her grave. It was directly ahead of them, in the second row.

Hamlet interrupted his thoughts. 'Perhaps they're together now.'

Horatio twitched, trying to respond. 'Do you think there's a heaven? And a hell?'

'If there's one there must be the other.'

'So you believe in them?'

Out here in the cold clear daylight Hamlet's answers were more natural. 'I don't know, I suppose I do. My family's so religious. They have to be.'

He picked up a handful of gravel from the path. Hunching his neck and shoulders into the collar of his coat he started pinging pebbles against headstones. Suddenly Horatio caught his hand with a strong grip.

Hamlet, unaccustomed to being touched, looked down at the white knuckles on the pale skin, the fist that held him so tightly. Then he realised. 'Was that your mother's grave? I'm sorry. I meant no disrespect.'

As Horatio released him Hamlet added, 'You're getting some muscle.'

They turned to walk on.

'You're strange,' Horatio said.

'I've had two fathers in four months, my uncle's suddenly my stepfather, my mother's my aunt-by-marriage, my cousins are my stepsisters, you think I should be normal after that?'

'But you've always been strange.' Horatio meant no disrespect either, but later he remembered saying it and was shocked at his boldness. To the crown prince!

They picked their way through the clods of mud and the holes in the ground, skirting the piles of muck and frozen human dung. The land around Elsinore was thinly grassed, and the moat dark and smelly. A dead swan floated near the bridge. Yet the grimness of the scene was relieved by the deep green of the pine forests and the intense white of the snow-capped mountains. From this direction, in this light, the lines of the castle seemed milder, giving it the air of a benign but shabby grandfather. The stone walls, weathered by rain and wind, were a soft grey. Horatio, son of a noble penniless family, eight years old when he arrived at Elsinore with his mother, he to be a companion for the prince and she the queen's lady-in-waiting, now thought of the ancient building as home.

They entered under the shadow of the portcullis. The gargoyles dripped like boys with runny noses. Vivid in red and orange, the guards raised their spears in salute. It seemed to Horatio that there was something sulky about them these days. Hamlet's father had been strict, but the soldiers respected him, and from respect for the father came respect for the son. Under the new king Claudius, standards were slipping.

The place was very quiet. A couple of servant girls went by, carrying bags of kitchen scraps from the kitchen. The girls nodded respectfully to Hamlet and giggled at Horatio. Laertes, son of the king's chief advisor, had told Horatio that two of the kitchen girls were 'easy', and he wondered now if these were the two. The plump one would be nice to kiss. But the other was lithe; her breasts looked firm, just the right size for his hands.

A greyhound loped behind the girls, following the scent of guts and bones in the bags. We should have taken Hamlet's dog with us, Horatio thought, knowing the creature was probably in its pen in the kitchen garden. Sometimes Hamlet seemed to forget the dog for days on end; Horatio loved dogs and wished he had his own.

One of the king's secretaries, smoking a pipe, stood talking to a man who had both arms folded and looked cross. They ceased their conversation and bowed to Hamlet, who frowned back at them. They ignored Horatio.

Neither boy spoke again until they were at the other side of the main courtyard. Horatio was about to suggest a game of billiards. But Hamlet said, 'See you tomorrow,' and went through the door to his own quarters.

Horatio nodded his reply too late: his friend was gone.

THREE

Three weeks after this Horatio and his cousin Bernardo stumbled into Hamlet's bedroom in the middle of the night. The long climb to the prince's apartment, up the difficult winding staircase, in the cold air, left them both panting. Several times they had been forced to stop and hold the candles away from their bodies, so their breath would not put out the brave little lights.

Why does he sleep up here? Bernardo wondered. He could have almost any room in the castle.

Bernardo, a farmer's son, understood only the practical. The bedroom should be close to the barn. A view was useful if it showed a storm approaching.

When a pig had to be slaughtered you sharpened your knife.

He was already churned up and confused by the night's events, which were outside the realm of his experience, beyond the limits of his imagination. The rush up the stairs gave him a pain in the stomach.

Horatio did not knock, just pushed open the door. It whinged and groaned. They tiptoed into the room.

Hamlet asleep was curled up like half of a puzzle. A large black dog took up the other side of the bed. The dog lifted his head, gazed at Horatio for a moment, then lay back down. But his eyes stayed open and he continued to watch the intruders.

Horatio hesitated. 'Do you think we should wake him?' he asked.

'Do you think we should be here at all?' Bernardo asked, trying to stop shaking. But when Horatio didn't answer he added, 'Go on.'

Bernardo was just inside the door. Horatio was closer to the bed. But Horatio still hesitated. He didn't know how to do it. He wanted to stroke Hamlet into gentle awareness but thought it would look too much like love. Instead he shook Hamlet's shoulder roughly, as if he were angry.

Hamlet sat up so suddenly that the other two

stepped back in surprise. The dog sat up with him, blinking and shaking its head. 'WHAT?' Hamlet shouted. His white hair was awry and his eyes stared at them but saw nothing. Then he focused and became awake. 'What the fuck do you want?'

Horatio laughed at the swearword.

'Sorry,' said Bernardo automatically.

'Well, what are you doing in here?' The prince frowned at Bernardo. 'Who are you anyway? Are you Bernardo?'

Both Horatio and Bernardo nodded.

Hamlet brushed back his hair and in the dim light of the two candles they saw his eyes, normally so pale a blue that they merged into grey, becoming sharper, glistening like a fox's. 'What's happened? Something's happened.'

Again words deserted Horatio. 'I don't know how to say it,' he confessed.

'I'll tell you,' Bernardo said, stepping forward.

Hamlet wouldn't take his gaze from Horatio. 'I want you to tell me,' he said, like a small boy.

'Do you believe in ghosts?'

'Yes.'

The sharpness and quickness of the reply startled Horatio even more. 'You…you do?'

'If it hurries you then, yes, I believe in ghosts.'

The dog slipped off the bed and slunk out the door to sit on the landing outside. Horatio sat on the end of the bed. Bernardo sucked in his breath at the daring of it, at the casual relationship that existed between the two. There were rumours about them, but Bernardo was not able to tell the truth from the queer tension that he felt in the room.

Hamlet was watching Horatio closely. The prince wore no top.

This room's so cold, Bernardo thought. He's tough all right.

'I didn't believe in ghosts. Never have,' Horatio said. He paused. 'And now I do.'

'So are you saying that you've seen a ghost? Tonight I suppose? Otherwise you wouldn't have woken me.'

Horatio stared at him. The flickering light of the candles in the dark draughty room made the prince's face almost demonic. Through the cloverleaf window in the stone wall Bernardo saw one distant star. Then it went out.

Hamlet was staring back at Horatio.

At last Horatio said, 'We think we saw your father.'

For a moment Hamlet did not move, did not break his gaze. Then he leapt from under the blankets. With incredible athleticism he turned in midair, like a white cat, and landed facing Bernardo, who hastily backed into the corridor. He found himself next to the dog, which was standing now, hairs bristling, as though it understood perfectly.

Hamlet came to the door. Bernardo stared into his terrible eyes. He felt the eyes were talking to him, not the voice. He heard the words, 'Did you see him too?' and he nodded.

F O U R

Outside the air hung with cold. The three boys scrunched along the terrace, in front of the throne room. Hamlet's dog loped close behind. The frost on the grass was so thick it could have been mistaken for snow.

'Maybe we'll see his footprints,' Horatio whispered. His words left his mouth in a balloon of steam and floated away across the lawns.

'Ghosts don't leave footprints,' Bernardo whispered back.

'How would you know?'

Hamlet had put on a white singlet to match the

white britches he slept in. Dressed in nothing more than that and a black cloak, and a pair of long black boots, he led them down the steps and along the path to the fountain of Neptune. Its water was frozen in a silent arc. A melancholy clock in the distance was striking, too many times for Bernardo to count. As he listened, the gongs started to sound out of tune and irregular, warped, vaguely disturbing. He hurried to catch up with the other two.

They were in the vast main courtyard, ten thousand metres square. Looking down on them were the closed and curtained windows of the royal apartments.

'Was it here?' Hamlet asked. It was the first time he had spoken since they had left his bedroom. His voice was croaky. The dog forced its way past the two boys and pressed in against Hamlet's legs. Horatio nodded.

Bernardo gazed around at the tall dark silent buildings. 'What's the dog's name?' he asked, looking down at the creature, which resembled a short-haired wolf.

The other two stared at him as if he were crazy. Neither of them answered. Bernardo blushed. The night was so still it might have been a painting. Then a large bird flew across the painting, its wings beating like sword blades. From upstairs somewhere came a thud, a door or a window shutter perhaps, but too far away to worry the boys.

'He mightn't come back tonight,' Horatio whispered, after fifteen minutes had passed. All three of them were turning into ice.

But just as he said 'tonight' Bernardo grabbed his arm. 'There he is.'

The boys huddled closer as the figure approached. He wore a full-length cloak, brown, heavy. His head was bare. Long silver hair blew wildly as though there were a strong wind, but the castle flags hung limp, and the leaves on the trees stayed undisturbed.

The man's facial features were hard to discern. He had two eyes, a nose, a mouth. No beard. His face was thin. As he passed a garden seat it seemed that he saw them. He stopped between a pair of huge stone lions and stared at them. He was about fifty metres away.

The black dog whined dolorously and sat on Hamlet's feet.

'Is it him?' Horatio asked Hamlet. 'It is him, isn't it?'

Hamlet didn't answer, just nodded. A full minute later he said, 'I think so.'

Bernardo gazed in rapture. He forgot to be scared. Here was one of the greatest events in the history of Denmark, surely, and he was intimately involved. Despite his confident words to the prince he had not been sure of what he had seen before. But if it were Hamlet's father, it was a ghost, and he, young Bernardo, son of a farmer from outside Gavatar, visiting Elsinore to spend a few months with his cousin Horatio, was witnessing what perhaps no one in the world had ever seen.

When the man made a motion with his arm, Bernardo jerked backwards as though he had been struck.

'What does he want?' Horatio muttered to Hamlet. They both ignored Bernardo.

'He wants me,' Hamlet said. 'Always did.'

The man motioned again.

Hamlet shook Horatio free and started walking towards the two lions.

'Come back,' Horatio hissed. 'Come back.' He ran a few urgent steps after his friend. 'You don't know what he'll do. He could kill you.'

But then he stopped, and the black dog lay down on the path beside him and whimpered.

Hamlet was aware of the sharpness of the night air, the gravel and the dead leaves that crackled like bones under his feet, the lonely cry of a distant curlew. He thought about the fresh grave he had stood coldly above, fewer than five months earlier. He recalled the clod of frozen earth he had tossed onto the coffin. He heard again the echo of the clod as it bounced off the wood, as though the box were hollow.

As Hamlet walked towards him, the man in the distance seemed to grow bigger. Somehow the boy was unafraid. Oh, he trembled but so did Horatio, so did Bernardo, so would anyone in the midnight cold. Only the man waiting, with the shadow of an alder tree across him, only he was still. And his hair had stopped blowing.

Hamlet got close enough to see him clearly, except for his face, which looked to be all stubble and eyes, white eyes that seemed to have no pupils. He noticed that the brown cloak had a thin red collar. Now Hamlet felt, if not frightened, then disturbed. In the months since the funeral the boy had forgotten most of his encounters with his father. During that time it was as though his mind concentrated on three images only: his father's terse smile when he gave him the long-legged chestnut colt, the proud hands he laid on his head when Hamlet won his first fight, and the gentle hands that picked him up one night and carried him to bed, when the boy was felled by influenza and went to the doorway of death, lingering a long time, as if he would pass through. As if he wanted to pass through. Then he had returned.

But this meeting, this strange encounter inbetween the two stone lions, brought back a flood of other memories: battles and beatings, painful lessons in riding, tests of strength, and cold hungry nights spent alone in his tower room, when Hamlet had failed those tests. For the first time the boy faltered. He wanted so much to show the silver in his veins. He wanted to be the size of a king, man enough for anything. But Horatio and Bernardo were far behind, out of hearing, the night was as cold as the tomb, and the man in front of him was rotten with death.

In spite of this the boy spoke. 'What do you want with me?'

His question was enshrouded with mist from his mouth, as though he had forced open a cranny to hell. He tried to make his voice sound strong, but it cracked on the last two words.

The man placed his left hand on the head of the lion. When he replied, Hamlet saw no mist of breath from his mouth. 'Pay attention to what I have to tell you.'

'I will.'

'I have come to speak to you one last time.'

'I am listening.'

'I am the spirit of your father.'

Hamlet could not open his mouth, could not take his eyes from the emaciated face, could not even nod for fear his head would fall off.

'By day I am condemned to twist in fire, until the sins of my life are burned away. And by night doomed to walk, for some short time yet.'

'I'm sorry indeed, sir,' Hamlet gasped.

'There is no need to pity me. I have not come here to torture you, to burn your ears with such stories. Indeed it is forbidden for me to talk about these matters to one who is of the earth. I have returned for another reason.'

'Then tell me.'

'If you ever loved your father…'

The man left the words hanging in the air and this time Hamlet was not able to speak, just nodded dumbly.

'If ever you did love your father, I call upon you now to take revenge.'

'Revenge?'

'I call upon you to avenge my foul and unnatural murder.'

The ghost growled the last word. Hamlet thought it the loudest sound he had ever heard.

'Murder?'

'Murder most foul.'

In agitation the man began to walk away from the lions, as if he did not know where he was going.

Hamlet stumbled after him. Behind him Horatio too started to walk, and further behind, Bernardo. The dog slunk away towards the eastern corner of the courtyard, then broke into a run, disappearing around the side of the library.

Bernardo wished he could hear the conversation

happening in front of him. What a story this would be to tell back in Gavatar. Perhaps Horatio could hear some of it, and would tell him later. Bernardo did not expect Hamlet to confide in him. But the boy did not like to get any closer. After all, it was his cousin who was Hamlet's friend, not him. Strange though, you'd think you'd hear their voices, on such a clear still night. But so far, not a word.

Hamlet had caught up with the figure of his father. In horror, desperate for details, he asked, 'But if you were murdered…how did it happen? Who would do such a thing?'

The ghost stopped and stared with his blank blind eyes. 'You know the story they tell of my death? That I was walking through the orchard and was bitten by a snake?'

'Yes!'

'The story has been believed from one end of the country to the other.'

'Of course.'

'I tell you, and mark the words well, it is a lie. A bloody and vicious lie, as bloody and vicious as the act of murder itself.'

Hamlet tried to ignore the hectoring tone, to force back the memories of his father's lectures in the past, to overcome the weakness that crept through his limbs when in the presence of his father alive.

'Then who…?'

'Know this, Hamlet. Know it well. The snake that bit me now wears my crown.'

The great voice that had once been a mighty roar was now a feeble wheeze. But the impact of the words was enough.

'My uncle!' Hamlet stammered. 'My uncle! Your brother!'

'No other.'

Hamlet, unable to continue in the presence of such drama, stared at his father, shaking his head. The man stared back for a few moments, then took another step, a half-step, that brought him terribly close to his son. Struggling to hold his ground Hamlet looked away, to the sky, to the castle.

'It was not enough that he seduced your mother,' the ghostly figure whispered. 'The woman I loved and trusted, and the man I shared my childhood with, the two people in the world who were closest to me! Betrayed by them both!'

'My mother,' said Hamlet, thinking at the same time: then I was not one of the people in the world closest to him?

He did not know which betrayal hurt him most.

His father showed no interest in how the fusillade of news was affecting his son.

Hamlet noticed something new now about the figure before him. It seemed to have faded and moved away, even though Hamlet could swear the man was still standing in front of him.

When the ghost spoke again his voice sounded vague and fretful. 'He killed me as I lay in the orchard. He poured poison into my ear.'

The young prince could think of nothing to say. His father was like an old man complaining that someone had taken one of his slippers. Yet he was talking about death. Death and murder.

'The night is fading away. I have a long way to travel. I leave you to your responsibility. I go to mine.'

Hamlet shook his head, not so much to stop the ghost leaving as to save his father a little longer from the awfulness of which he had spoken. He reached out with his right arm. But without success. In front of his eyes the ghost evaporated. For a few moments there was a smell, obnoxious to the nose, sulphur mixed with the mustiness of his father alive, then not even that.

Hamlet, frozen to the spot, had to be turned and made to walk and talk and breathe again by Horatio and Bernardo. It was as though he had gone through a door to some terrible place and they had to reach through it themselves to pull him back. The excitement they felt earlier was gone; now they were frightened for the prince. They plied him with questions to which he made no reply. 'Was it your father? Did he speak to you? Did you say anything? He looked like he was talking! What did he say? Were you scared? Why did he come here? Does he want something of you?'

S I X

Her Majesty Queen Gertrude was looking up at her new husband, and at the same time fingering the pepper pot. She appeared as glacial as ever, her fair skin coldly beautiful, her eyes steady. Her hair, hinting of red, was swept back from her face, giving her a high forehead, and allowing her strong clear eyes to meet the gaze of anyone in the room.

Some forty guests were seated around the table in the state dining room, not the great hall used for official banquets, but the less formal one on the ground floor of the royal apartments. Pale sunlight through the stained glass windows cast colours from hunting scenes on the king's face, but all the warmth in the room came from the log fires burning in vast fireplaces at each end.

The luncheon was over, and Claudius's speech was drawing to an end. Bearded, beefy, red-faced, slightly hoarse, he was not a natural orator, more at home in the hunting field, but he had a forceful style of speaking that commanded respect. Shorter than most men, yet with a big head, he compensated for his height by standing on his toes, leaning forwards as though he were looking for a fight. He was fifty years old, balding, with watery eyes, yet Claudius still had a sensual quality that attracted women, in a way that his dignified older brother had never understood.

On the king's other side was Polonius, his chief advisor. Polonius gazed steadily at Claudius. His expression was composed and calm. His hands were in his lap. Although he had written the speech, he listened to it now with the demeanour of a man who was weighing every word.

Horatio, at the foot of the table, trying to look interested in Claudius, took a moment to look around. He noticed Gertrude's unconscious fiddling with the pepper pot and wondered at it. She had always been so punctilious when it came to table etiquette. She snapped at him or Hamlet when they fidgeted during speeches. Especially Hamlet. 'You will have to listen to thousands of speeches,' she had told him. 'Many of them boring. But the fate of Denmark may one day depend on your manners. A yawn at the wrong moment can be a grave insult.'

Polonius was the exemplar today, Horatio thought. Not a flicker of movement. Other men his age were beginning to tremble but not Polonius. Those sharp eyes and big ears had seen and heard many secrets, and his crafty brain processed them to his advantage. He had served five kings, and each one had found him indispensable.

I bet he was an old man when he was twenty, Horatio thought. Not so many wrinkles maybe, but I can't see him playing football or getting drunk or going in a farting competition. The thought made him smile.

Polonius's son, Laertes, was only seventeen but already a hard drinker and a keen fighter. He was away in France studying. 'If Polonius knew half of what Laertes got up to…' Horatio had said to Hamlet a couple of days earlier. To which Hamlet had grumpily replied, 'Polonius knows everything.'

Opposite Horatio were Rosencrantz and Guil-denstern, two young men who hung around the court trying to eke out a living by picking up minor missions. They had been favourites of Hamlet's grand-mother. Since her death they lacked patronage, but Claudius seemed to be growing fonder of them every day. Never seen apart, they could have been twins: Rosencrantz dark, Guildenstern blond, both lean, tall, sharp-faced, and always exquisitely dressed. Horatio did not know them well but he knew that he did not like them. They wore too much jewellery and he had the feeling they were laughing at his country manners when they whispered to each other, their mouths hidden by their elegantly manicured hands.

On Horatio's left was Osric. A friend of the king's, Osric was one of the new men who could be found everywhere at court these days. He was a rich young farmer whose only virtue was that he owned a lot of dirt, but he would rather be in the middle of the glitter and fun of court life than supervising gnarled old farmhands who grunted a couple of times a day and spent their nights in a drunken stupor induced by potato vodka. Tall and awkward, fair-haired and blue-eyed, he could have been good-looking but his eyes never stayed in the one place for more than a moment. He twitched when anyone spoke to him. Giggling at Claudius's jokes, wiping greasy hands on the tablecloth, standing and stretching across the table to take another portion of venison, Osric was uncouth in a way that Horatio, who was naturally courteous, could never be. Yet Osric's clothes were elaborate and expensive, and his manner exaggerated. In the presence of food he regressed.

Beside Osric was Ophelia, daughter of Polonius. She gazed at the king as though entranced by his every word, but Horatio found it difficult to believe that she was interested in the details of the new treaty with Lithuania. Ophelia's white-haired beauty seemed to derive from a secret spring inside her. Occasionally, when they were children playing together, Horatio had realised with a shock how beautiful she was. Most of the time he saw her just as a girl, a person, a friend, someone his own age. But then he would catch a glimpse of her and stop as if turned to stone, hardened by her perfection.

Horatio felt awkward when he was with her alone, though. She seemed always beyond his reach. In sunlight she was sunlight; in darkness she was shadow. It made conversation with her difficult for the unimaginative young man. How was it that Hamlet struck a fire from her that he could not? What magic did the prince bring that sparked her, yes, and other girls too, and made Horatio feel dull, clumsy, something of a brute who might always be left with the plainer girls.

Now, though, gnawing on a chicken bone, Horatio preferred to watch Hamlet. The young prince was tracing a design on the stiff linen tablecloth with a knife. Every few moments he pushed back a strand of white hair that kept falling over his eyes. Horatio was troubled by his expression. The prince's face, always fair, was now pale and anxious.

What happened that night the ghost appeared? If only Hamlet had said something, there in the court-yard, as they tried to make him walk and talk again. Or as they took him back towards his bedroom. But he had brushed away their excited questions, pausing only at the base of the tower to swear them both to silence, which he did in exhaustive detail.

'Swear you will say nothing.'

'Swear you will give no hint.'

'Swear you won't go around saying, "I know something about Hamlet but I'm not going to tell you."'

'Now swear you won't say things like, "I could tell you why he's being so strange but I'm not allowed to."'

He added, 'It's not enough that you must keep

this secret, but you must keep it secret that you know a secret.'

Then he had closed the door in their faces and climbed the stairs to his eyrie. Bernardo and Horatio were left in the cold and dark, baffled and angry.

'We were the ones who saw him,' Bernardo said. 'And now he won't even tell us.'

'It is his father though,' Horatio muttered. In his heart he agreed with Bernardo, but Bernardo was just a visitor, a farmboy who did not understand the complexities of rank, and besides, Horatio's first loyalty was to Hamlet. That was the stronger friendship. Even so, when Bernardo did not reply, he added weakly, 'Still, you're right, he could have said something.'

Since that night, Hamlet had been odd, even more odd than usual. Most of the time he seemed to be avoiding Horatio, but then would suddenly accost him with a wild speech about the moon, or asparagus, or hopscotch.

Nobody could accuse the new king of such eccentricity, Horatio thought, settling in his chair to listen to the end of the speech. Claudius was calm, considered, very much in control. He'd just announced the opening of talks with the old king of Norway, to stop the young Norwegian prince Fortinbras from launching attacks on Denmark's borders. Earlier he'd promised to lower interest rates, increase employment, build better roads and hospitals, and reduce taxes.

But now, with the official business out of the way, he turned to his nephew, the young man who had become his stepson.

Hearing his name called, Hamlet jerked in his seat like a harpooned seal. Around the room others stirred from their languor.

'What?' Hamlet asked rudely, staring straight at the king.

Claudius smiled indulgently. 'I merely ask, is there anything we here can do for you, we who are your friends, the people who love you most, and have your interests at heart? I fear the clouds still hang heavily over you, my dear Hamlet.'

Before the boy could answer Gertrude joined the conversation. 'It is time for you to lift your head again, my child, to stop seeking your dead father in the dust of the earth. All who live must die, and your father too has begun his journey into eternity. Of course everyone here grieves for him, but heavens above, my dear boy, the time comes to move on.'

Hamlet shrugged and looked at the wall opposite, at an oil painting of Joseph of Arimathea.

'Your sad manner shows a sweetness in you, Hamlet,' the king continued, 'that you felt such love for your father, but it also shows a stubbornness that is not so admirable. After all, your father lost his father, Hamlet, and that father lost his, and he his, and so on. These are the laws of God and of nature. For you to spend so long mourning is to spit in the face of God, of nature and of the dead themselves. Come now, what do you say?'

'What do I say?' Hamlet stared around him, as if he had seen none of these people before.

Horatio leaned forward. He was ready to leap from his seat if Hamlet did anything…but that was ridiculous. This wasn't some primitive domain of uncivilised warlords. Hamlet always knew the right thing to say. As if he would ever do anything that was…

'What do I say? Why sir, I say that nothing is good or bad, unless thinking makes it so.'

There was an embarrassed pause, broken by Claudius's awkward laugh. 'Well, that's neatly put. Now Hamlet, your mother has a special request to make of you.'

'Yes,' Gertrude said, taking her cue. 'Yes, indeed. Hamlet, it is our wish that you do not go back to boarding school for the next semester but that you stay here with us, close by our side.'

Hamlet gazed at her for so long that it was as if he had never seen his mother before.

'Very well,' he said at last. 'If that is your wish.'

'Good!' the king said, 'Good! That's what we like to hear. Everyone in agreement. That's how it should be. Come on now, drink up. No more speeches. Let's adjourn to the billiards room.'

SEVEN

Ophelia lay on the bed in her over-heated room. In summer this room was a nightmare but everyone envied her in winter.

The room had been freshly painted white. Ophelia, helped by Hamlet and her brother Laertes, had done the work herself. They were the world's messiest painters. One bright afternoon Hamlet, with the daring smile she found so attractive, had flicked a string of white drops onto her white dress. Looking down and finding herself bespattered she went to retaliate, but Laertes was there before her, defending his sister's honour. He was older than Hamlet, and often dour, but a light kind of madness had seized Laertes that day, and the two boys, wielding their long paintbrushes as swords, fenced from one end of the room to the other, Ophelia laughing even as she begged them to stop. Hamlet had turned to her, smiled, and said, 'I will, but only if you give me a...'

She never found out how the sentence was going to end. Laertes stabbed Hamlet from behind with his brush and so the battle resumed. They did not give up until the floor was slippery with the wet paint they had spilt. At last they agreed to a draw. Ophelia was left wondering what kind of forfeit Hamlet had been about to propose. Her instincts told her. And she would have given it, yes, gladly, would have pressed her lips to his, had it not been for Laertes' presence. She had been sulky with her brother afterwards, and he in turn had been over-friendly. As if he knew exactly what he had done.

It took them days to get the paint off their bodies. A large rug now covered the spots on the floor.

Lying on the bed and remembering, Ophelia smiled. What did she feel for Hamlet? she asked herself, not for the first time. What was it that caught and twitched within her at the thought of his eyes? Flickering in her mind was the image of a fish spinning through water, hooked but not taken, a naked silver body streaming wet.

She ran her fingers up the inside of her right thigh and gave a little cry at the silver lines left on her skin. Her nightdress felt too hot, too heavy. She slipped it off and lay back, panting at the heat, the exertion, the thoughts. Her fingers touched there again. Why did being naked feel so good? What would Hamlet look like naked?

She had seen him and Horatio a month or so back, the two boys shirtless, chopping wood in the kitchen yard behind the castle. They had grabbed the axes and sent the servants packing. She watched avidly from her window. Horatio had more muscle but Hamlet was the prettier. They were competing to chop the logs in the fewest number of strokes. How the silver blades had flashed in the sun! How the chips had scattered! And how the drops of sweat shone as they flew through the air.

As she gazed from behind her curtain, Ophelia had imagined them naked, tried to picture Hamlet naked and swinging that axe, had felt faint at the thought, had tried to stop her mind from dreaming such things, had finally been forced to drop the curtain back into place and rush from the room.

These were the thoughts she was unable to express to anyone, even to her confessor.

Lying there in the little room Ophelia thought she would go mad. Sweat trickled from her armpits; she groaned and growled as she touched herself again, and again tried to push back the forbidden pictures that threatened to crowd all else from her mind.

The interruption, when it came, was brutal and rude. It was her father, outside the door. Polonius sounded like the dull dry voice of death. 'What are you doing in there Ophelia?'

She struggled to find a voice. The sound that came from her throat was raspy. 'Doing?'

The handle rattled. 'What are you doing? Open this door. I know what you're doing. Open up I say.'

'Nothing. I'm doing nothing. I'm coming, I'm coming now.'

EIGHT

At exactly the same time Hamlet was perched on the highest point of the castle, a tower built to look out over the plains. If the armies of Norway came marching, Hamlet's father had wanted to be sure of a good view.

Behind him was the graveyard, the frozen river, the wastelands, and beyond them the meagre village of Clennstein. But Hamlet stared at the plains. A low heavy layer of dark clouds sat in the east, glooming the sky. He looked to the south. Down the valleys ran the conifers, straight lines pointing out of the creases and folds, pointing towards the distant bushy forest.

But if the massed armies of northern Europe had at that moment been galloping in close order straight towards the castle the young prince would not have seen them. His mind was a chaos of emotions. The infidelities of his mother, the treachery of his uncle, the distracting beauty of Ophelia and, over it all, the shadow of his father.

Even that shadow was split, fragmented like a humourless harlequin suit, into the towering figure of the powerful king, the severe patriarch, the occasionally kind father, and now the forbidding and ghastly ghost.

Hamlet felt there was no room for himself. He had been crowded out of his own mind. He struggled to find something solid, something beautiful. He wanted to be a continent, not an archipelago. There were the two men, father and uncle, father and stepfather, king and king, man and man.

Hamlet looked down. The tower was so high that as he looked at the ground it seemed to start moving, moving faster, accelerating. The young prince felt giddy. His stomach began to turn over. He looked away at the gullies again. He felt so small on the top of the tower, like a flea on a horse, a slight live thing on this tower of rock. He knew the wind could blow him away on a whim.

The charge his father had laid on him: the king had come back from death to rule his son, so that once again nothing existed in Hamlet's life but the decrees of the father, one man using the boy to attack and destroy another man. It was a mammoth fighting a mammoth, using the boy as the weapon.

Hamlet trembled. For a moment he tasted the knowledge that he would not survive this. He felt his mind becoming paper, then torn-up paper, then burnt paper, then ashes, and he sensed too the coming annihilation of his body.

He slipped down from the tower, through the great courtyard, out of the castle, into the fields, running in circles. Against the rich green grass and the close horizon, the lowering clouds, pregnant with storm and snow, against the white windmill and the stone tower, Hamlet was all that moved. His white hair and white shirt held the eye; a line could be drawn between him and the windmill and the dark tower, the last two heavy and immovable, the other too light, too bright: nothing to hold it to the earth. He slipped in the mud and rolled down the hill but was up again as he spun, flitting, flying. He was alive and hopeless.

In her room Ophelia sat on her bed, waiting for something to happen. The door was open. Her father had demanded that it stay open. Polonius made many demands. There were rules for everything. Be careful of boys. Don't lend money. Don't borrow money. Keep away from Hamlet. Dress modestly. Don't speak out, stay in the background, don't gossip. Don't believe Hamlet when he flirts with you.

Polonius was so much older than the fathers of her friends. He wanted to control everything she did. She felt as closely watched as a valuable broodmare coming into season.

She wandered down the corridor. This was the oldest wing of the castle, and the tiles on the floor were chipped and worn. Once they had been bright and lively but now they were dull, grimy even. Nothing seemed to be cleaned properly anymore. The servants were getting so slovenly.

Ophelia heard the soft voice of Reynaldo, an effete young man who had tutored Laertes at his university in Heidelberg. But it seemed Polonius was doing most of the talking. They were in her father's drawing room. No doubt Polonius had Reynaldo bailed up in the corner of the stiff leather couch, the way he liked to do when he wanted to control someone. Ophelia had huddled into that corner many times as Polonius sat inches from her, croaking urgent admonitions into her sullen ears.

She stopped for a moment then drifted closer. The voices played together, one winding in and out of the other. Polonius's harsh monologues contrasted with Reynaldo's gentle tones. They were whispering like conspirators. She heard her father say, 'The way to do it is to get to know his friends a little.'

'His friends?' Reynaldo asked.

'Yes, yes, of course, it's the best way. You get to know them, then you bring his name into the conversation one day.'

'Mention his name, yes?'

'Very casually, mind you. "Oh, you probably know Laertes", that kind of thing.'

'Yes. Just mention that I tutored him last year. And I'm interested in how he's going.'

'Exactly. You could say that you're a friend of the family, then you lead them on.'

'Lead them on?'

'You say something like, "He's a bit wild, isn't he? Smoking, drinking, that kind of thing?"'

'I see. Just a little prompt. That's clever.'

'And then if they say, "Oh, yes, you should have

seen Laertes the other day, lucky his father doesn't find out what he gets up to, and so on and so on," why then, you write to me. At once. Most urgently.'

In the cold corridor Ophelia trembled and drew her wrap closer around her. Her hair, a kind of transparent white, like icicles, flowed around her face, making her look even colder.

'And is it just smoking and drinking? Are they the things you're worried about? Because you know how boys are at university…of course they get up to a bit of mischief. There's no great harm in some of the things they…especially when they first arrive. They can be a bit naughty, away from home for the first time, but it doesn't always…'

'Oh no. Not just smoking and drinking. No indeed. Cheating in his exams. Drugs. Promiscuity.'

'Promiscuity?'

'Yes! Is he picking up girls, playing with them, you know the sort of thing. They're all sex-mad at that age. I know what they're like. Those boys, with their hormones going crazy, wanting to press their bodies into the girls, it's all they think of. Touching them. Feeling them. And worse. They can't control themselves. They get the girl naked, and before you know it…they can't help themselves. They're diseased with lust. Whores. Is he whoring around? I'll stake money that he is. They'll know him at the whorehouses, depend on it.'

'Sir, really, I'm not sure…I think you're being harsh on your son. I think his basic character is good.'

'Good character, rubbish. If you knew his mother…The two of them are stamped with her mark. Oh yes, I know what to look for. I'm always having to talk to Ophelia about her behaviour. She's ripening, you know. You can tell…the way she cavorts with the prince. He may be a prince but that doesn't make him immune from the sex drive. In fact I think he's oversexed. Oh yes. I know the type…'

Ophelia fled. Her hair streamed behind her. She ran to the end of the corridor, then back again, then the same, then again, backwards and forwards, a desperate trapped thing, panting and wild-eyed. She ran into her cell and went straight to the window, gripping the frame and staring down into the courtyard. Oh she could fly, she could soar from the sill and be a white bird, and everyone down there would look up and wonder, drop their swords and their pots and their mops and call out to each other and to her, 'Ophelia, is it you? Ophelia? Oh see see the beautiful Ophelia, she flies!'

She heard a voice behind her, a hoarse, light whisper. She thought she heard the word 'flying'. She turned fast, ready to kick and bite if she had to.

It was Hamlet. He looked as wild and confused as she felt. He stared at her with huge eyes, as if he had expected to find someone else in the room. His mouth was open, he was gasping for breath, and his chest shook. Was he having an asthma attack? But asthma did not explain the state of his clothes. His jacket was open and his shirt half torn off. She saw his smooth brown skin and a dark nipple. His jeans were smeared with grass stains and his boots bruised with mud, black mud, almost purple in places.

'My lord…' she stammered. He snarled at her, showing his teeth. 'What is it?' she said, afraid of her father. 'You shouldn't be here.'

Hamlet stood there, panting. He seemed to be calming down. He took a step closer. She did not back away. He studied her face with the greatest intentness. It was as though he wanted to memorise her appearance. He continued down her body, to her breasts. Now it was Ophelia's turn to breathe hard. She felt a pressure there, then a warmth. She felt the pressure most strongly in her nipples, as if his hands were resting on them. She blushed and was almost relieved when his gaze moved further down.

'My lord…' she murmured. She knew she should move but she couldn't. She wished he would say something but was scared at what he might say.

In the long dark corridor that led to the basement, at the appointed time, Hamlet met Ophelia. She wore white, like a frail bride, who could be borne away on a breeze. He wore black jeans and a black shirt. They quivered to see each other. Ophelia could have turned back, back through the door, back into the girls' court-yard. The light from that place fell behind her and the door was still closing.

Hamlet could have returned to the cellar where he had stored his toys, the relics of his past.

The thoughts flitted out of their minds again, like tiny fast moths. They continued walking and met, and began an elaborate dance. Ophelia clasped her arms to her thin body and revolved around him. He turned with her as his arms moved in a dance of their own. She spoke first: her voice was low and husky. 'Are you all right? Why do you haunt these dark places?'

'Why not? There's nothing above the ground. Is there?'

This was so much in accord with her own thoughts that it frightened her. She did not want her fears confirmed. 'Is this all there is then? I wanted more,' she said.

'It's hard when you are a bird who lives underground.'

'Birds can't live underground.'

'No, they can't.'

She stood still then and so did he.

'Can we live? Can we live at all?' she asked. Her voice echoed, bouncing off the brick-lined walls.

'Yes, it comes down to that. And to what comes after.'

'To what?' She didn't understand him.

'Why, whether we are to live or not to live. To dance or to die. To breathe the painful air, or to sleep.'

'To sleep?'

'To stand in the shallows with a sword to fight the

surf, or to let the waves wash you away.' He took her by the elbow and leaned closer to her ear and whispered into it. 'To be or not to be.'

She was frightened and pulled away and could not listen to him.

'To stay under here for ever?' she asked. Her voice was tinny and thin, almost disdainful. Fear was corrupting her.

'It would be easy,' he said. For a moment he sounded almost bored. 'So easy to do it. It's what happens afterwards, that's the thing.'

She put her hands to her ears and tried to say 'stop it', but could not.

'If it was my father, if he told the truth, if he twists in fire, if he the murdered one twists in fire, what's there for the one who murders himself? No sleep for him I think, no peace, not for a long time. Torment for him, I think.'

The tunnel felt colder and colder to Ophelia. She tried to concentrate on Hamlet's twin thoughts, the references to his father, the references to death. His voice went on, soft, in the darkness.

'Why would anyone put up with it all? The cruelty, the injustice, the frustration, the pangs and the pain. The love that's not returned. After all, the ticket to that undiscovered country is cheap enough. A bare knife will get you there. Surely we'd all fly to it at once if we thought we could have perfect peace there, protected forever.'

Hamlet walked away a dozen paces and turned to face Ophelia again. Looking straight at her he said, 'It's the same with everything. I don't pick up the knife because I think about it too much and the thinking paralyses my arm. Action is hot, and thought is cold. Action is courage and reflection is cowardly. Picking up the knife has the colours of truth. As soon as I hesitate, the scene takes on a sickly hue.'

'My father told me to keep away from you. That you are not to be trusted.'

She wanted to see him hot. She wanted him to talk about her. What he felt. What he wanted. The future for them. An expression came to his face but it went again before she could see what it was. The darkness made it difficult. The darkness and the distance and the dance.

Hamlet shrugged. 'Why then, you had better go. Do what your father tells you.'

'But I don't want to.'

Suddenly with a great roar he ran towards her. She thought he was going to run her down. But he went straight past, and fifty metres down the corridor turned left. She heard his boots clattering up the staircase and then the noise was gone and the silence in the corridor became complete.

T E N

Hamlet's mental map had changed year by year. As he and Horatio had reached ten, eleven, twelve, the map increased in size, at the same time as it incorporated new landmarks. Now it extended to the farmlands, the forest, the villages. And within the castle it was no longer defined by his mother's suite of rooms, or the corner of the kitchen where the kind cook kept biscuits, or the sheltered courtyard where his nurse had taken him to play.

When he moved bedrooms at fourteen, the tower room became the centre of his map, and three important lines ran from it. One went down the staircase with the shiny handrail, which he slid down every day, then down a narrow darker set of steps that led to a small back door. This gave the quickest exit from the castle.

The second line wound its way to the southern wing, where old Polonius lived with his faithful son Laertes and his feckless daughter Ophelia.

The third was the line of routine, the daily route of breakfast room, school room, duelling hall, dining hall, art room, a route that most days the young prince followed with little thought.

There was a fourth line too, a secret line, that Hamlet lied to himself about. Were the map ever to be drawn, this route might appear as a series of faint dots, like an unmade road, or a horse trail across the mountains. Much of the time it was invisible, though it was more likely to be seen at night. It started in the tower room, like the others, and like them it went down the stairs. From there it led onto the roof and across the ridges and valleys, pausing near Ophelia's window, where the girl could sometimes be seen, by the light of the one mean candle her father allowed her.

Oh yes, she could be seen all right, seen as the white slip slid down her body, seen stretching, arms above her head, as she danced the pale nightgown down her body. Could be seen bending to the candle, her face glowing in its sweet light, her swollen lips open to blow the room into darkness. Even after the darkness she could be seen, in Hamlet's fevered mind, the swelling breasts and the smooth legs, the soft crack: he saw all but the pink light between her legs.

From there Hamlet would creep on past the servants' wing, watching for the assistant cook with the huge prick, the oafish nineteen-year-old stroking himself on his palliasse, in the dimness of the candle his cock casting a giant shadow on the wall. Hamlet stared at the shadow as much as he did at the cock, wondering and wishing, excited by the awful sight.

Down to a small window, in the shape of a slice of bread, where he would make his exit into the kitchen gardens, but before that he passed the room of one of the scullery maids. Forty or more years old, breasts like bags filled with water, genitals lost in her giant thighs, the triangle of hair spreading high up her navel, standing every night in the galvanised iron tub, obsessed with cleanliness, washing herself with dreamy concentration. The boy felt a deep hunger as he gazed at her. He could never feed at those breasts, could never satisfy her with his little thing. She always in the room, he always outside it. Always in the past, never in the future.

Then through the window to the staircase, down the stone steps, through the green door and into the squares of carrots and peas, potatoes and pumpkins, beetroot and squash. Some squares weeded and neat, others unkempt or barren. Around the perimeters, a hundred metres away in any direction, the pens of chickens, ducks, geese, the sheds of pigs, the huts where tools were kept.

In this strange land, in this tiny kingdom of pigs and turkeys, of beans and berries, the grotesque was not unknown. In this controlled world of moon at night and sun by day, of rain and snow and frost and summer warmth, Garath—always first to emerge from his hovel, Garath, the man charged with the care of the kitchen gardens—occasionally found hens strangled and sows stabbed, vines ripped down and soft fruit plucked and trampled.

The garden boys learned not to speak of this, not to speculate, just to obey Garath's grim orders: 'Strip the birds and scorch the sows, bury the fruit and restore the vines.'

Garath sent the meat to the kitchen but he did not eat it himself.

This is where the fourth line of Hamlet finished.

ELEVEN

And so time strode onwards, and Hamlet became older, filling into the body and shape of a young man, no longer an adolescent. Yet still he did nothing. Horatio was called away to do his first phase of army duty. Bernardo's father inherited a bigger farm, near Olsbrook, and the family moved there. The young man had not visited his cousin in Elsinore for a long time, and his memories of the night with Hamlet and Horatio and the spirit were becoming uncertain.

Laertes finished university in France and went to England, to study military tactics.

Hamlet and Ophelia were the only constants.

They never went away. Within the walls of the great grey castle they had no one but each other. Ophelia lived and breathed Hamlet. She disappeared into Hamlet. She gave herself to him in every way but the one she wanted. If Hamlet smiled and spoke to her, she was happy. If he frowned or appeared not to notice her she did not want to live. There was nothing to do in the castle, no new people, an angry king and a fretful queen, grumbling mumbling muttering servants, tired old men and boring young ones. Hamlet was the salmon in the river, the balloon on the breeze, the new moon silvering the sky. He was quickness and light, a shadow on a wall, an illusion, a dream, a fancy. He was a glimpse, nothing solid. How could she anchor her boat to a wave? Yet that was what she wanted.

Hamlet's behaviour was becoming more and more odd. Even the soldiers whispered about it. He was so beautiful that no one wanted to notice. Illness of that kind was for others, not for the beautiful or the rich or the royal. It seemed impossible. Yet he spoke in a way that often made no sense: if he entered a conversation his words jumped and skipped and went backwards, or a year forwards.

It made people uncomfortable and made Ophelia

angry and miserable. He needed her, she could help him, if he took the comfort she alone could give, then he would wax not wane, he would laugh and spring around and be the powerful potent prince he had once promised to become. He would be the full moon, shining so strongly over the land that all would kneel before him, and she, she would be content as his Venus, the brightest star in the sky, but only a star.

She would give him everything, didn't he understand that? Did she have to spell it out for him? That was the one thing she could not do. He could have it but she would not be whorish. He must find it himself and then, expecting resistance, he would be moved and delighted and grateful to find her open. Oh how open she would be! Everything would be his. She would be his. Let him use her as the means to his fulfilment, did he not understand the gift that lay waiting and panting and bleeding and ready?

She was huge with her readiness and openness and generosity. Did he not understand that she lay naked on her bed every night, made huge by her willingness? How could he, at the top of the tower, in his room made of stone, not feel the waves of her openness radiating through the castle? Wouldn't the servants toss restlessly in their sleep as the waves flowed into them? Would not the animals in their pens grunt and groan with uneasy recognition? How then could a prince, the most beautiful boy in the land, the boy strung as sensitively as a violin, not be drawn to her, drawn to her room, by the energy with which she shone for him?

TWELVE

'Do you believe ghosts?' Hamlet asked.

Horatio was back at Elsinore, after his first period of military service. He stood a lot taller but had lost weight; perhaps because of the poor food the soldiers were given, perhaps because he was growing so fast. With him was Laertes, cool and aloof now, patronising to the younger men, and resentful that he was not still in London.

Hamlet was pleased to see Laertes, delighted to see Horatio. He eyed his friend affectionately, noting the new confidence in his posture, the easy way he wore his clothes. Horatio's mushroom-brown hair was cut short, and he had the stubble of a beard, but his honest dark eyes held the same regard and loyalty for Hamlet as they always had.

The two of them went walking down a long wide strip of grass, each with a racquet. They had invented a game which all the young officers had picked up and now played with eager devotion. It was simple enough— hitting a hard little ball they'd made by binding a stone with thin cord. The aim was to get it into holes they'd drilled in the ground, five holes in all.

Horatio paused at his friend's question. Staring down at the wet grass, he shook his head, puzzled. 'Do I believe in ghosts? Haven't we already had this conversation?'

'No, not "Do you believe in ghosts?" I said, "Do you believe ghosts?"'

'I don't follow you.'

'You should Horatio, you should. But my question is, if a ghost tells you something, can it be believed?'

'I don't know.' Horatio had found his ball and he lined up his next shot. He was getting more interested now. Perhaps Hamlet was about to talk about that extraordinary night on the battlements, the night that remained a dark spot between them.

The night that had triggered a new Hamlet, a changed Hamlet.

Horatio hit his ball. It flew for a couple of long moments then hit a tree and dropped to the ground. He turned back to Hamlet.

'I don't know,' he said again, but slowly, now taking the question seriously. 'Where are ghosts sent from? If from the devil, then it would be reasonable to disbelieve everything they say. I hope you're not suggesting we should trust Satan's emissaries.'

They walked on.

'Yes, but having escaped the devil's clutches for a while,' Hamlet said, 'they might speak the truth. Perhaps they slip away from the underworld in order to do so. After all, do they not generally encourage virtue in those to whom they appear?'

'The stories seem to have it that way,' Horatio admitted. 'I've never heard of a ghost telling someone to do wrong. But what is the difference between a ghost and an evil spirit? Haven't we gone past your ball?'

'Have we? I can't remember where it landed.'

'Near that alder, no?'

They combed through the grass with their racquets. Hamlet, however, did not seem to have his mind on the job. 'And,' he said, 'it is also possible that the ghost has come from nowhere because he has not yet gone anywhere. Suppose he is condemned to walk the earth's mantle for a time? He is under the influence of neither divinity nor Satan.'

'Is that what he told you?' Horatio asked boldly, meeting the prince's eye.

Hamlet blushed but did not answer. Instead he pressed Horatio harder. 'If it were so, would you believe such a ghost?'

'I might. If I were convinced that the thing meant me no harm.'

'Hmmm. So it comes down to that. It always comes down to that.'

'To what?'

'Oh to oneself, always to oneself. There are more things in heaven and earth than are dreamt of in your philosophy, Horatio, or in mine, but somehow we are expected to make it all intelligible, to carve statues from air and make books from bark. It is too much. This is the proper work of gods and we are not gods, indeed all our human errors come from the vain belief that we are.'

'Here's your ball,' Horatio said.

THIRTEEN

Hamlet dreamed of Ophelia. He had hard dreams of her, and soft ones. He dreamed in prepositions: beside, with, on top of, under, in, out. The dreams were unbearable sometimes, they sent him crazy, but he could not stop them nor did he want to. There were times when he went to the corridor that ran to her room but it always seemed something thwarted him, or conditions were not right, and on more than one occasion he bumped into her father. It was as though Polonius lurked near her bedroom, ubiquitous, insidious and obsequious. 'Why, Highness, taking the night air, such a fragrant night is it not, would you care to share a sherry?'

On these occasions, Hamlet, struggling not to blush, as anxious to repudiate the sherry as he was to obscure his greed for the beautiful Ophelia, tried to pretend it was mere coincidence that found him in this part of the castle, and he went away furious at his loss of dignity. Behind him he left the old man, triumphant, rampant, smug with the knowledge that once more he had chased away the cocky young invader. The fortress remained inviolate. Behind her door Ophelia tossed and turned and moaned, not hearing the stubborn men outside.

But the night came when Hamlet went right to the door of her bedroom, penetrated the outermost chamber and stood with hand upon the knob, knowing that if he opened this, the final door…what? He realised that he knew nothing of what would happen. Breathing painfully, he tried to imagine Ophelia starting up from her bed, with pale fingers to her throat, frightened but perhaps also…what? If she cried for help, if she screamed, if she flung accusations at him, if she complained of him the next day, if she ran from him in fear, if she fainted, if she coldly told him to leave, if she became ill with loathing at the sight of him…

Feeling faint himself he turned the knob but somehow could not push against the reluctant door to open it. He gripped tightly, disgusted at his lack of resolve. Polonius was not the problem this time. The old man was nowhere to be seen. The problem had to be in himself. He knew what he wanted but he could not take it. Then he heard the noise of someone coming down the corridor. Ark. He made a sound like a crow. Letting go of the knob he slunk back and hid behind a harpsichord, like a thief. Laertes entered the chamber, soft but sure. Leaving at dawn to return to London, he had come to say goodbye. He went straight to the bedroom door, opened it, and, with the complete confidence that only a brother can possess towards a sister, went inside.

Hamlet groaned and writhed and wailed and gnashed his teeth. He wanted the insouciance of a brother and the ardour of a lover. He crept away down the long lonely empty corridor, climbed back up to his cold tower room, with nothing but his own hands to hug him, nothing but himself to keep him warm.

F O U R T E E N

Everyone in Elsinore welcomed the news that a well-known troupe of actors had arrived at the castle. It was unusual to see them so far from their homes. Normally they performed at a theatre at the other end of the country, but now business was poor and they were reduced to shuffling their way around Denmark town by town. This appearance at the residence of the royal family was the last of their tour.

Hamlet had seen them frequently. He knew them well. They were favourites of his. Watching them approach, however, from his position on the parapet, he was at first too distracted by his own confusion to wonder what entertainment they brought. 'There is more tragedy here than they could show us on a stage,' he thought. 'Here at Elsinore the play becomes real, the drama haunts us every moment of our lives.'

Suddenly he changed his mind. Jumping up from his squatting position with an acrobatic leap, he went looking for them.

The members of the group were milling around in the main entrance hall, waiting for lodgings to be found, rooms to be made ready. Hamlet counted eleven, all men and boys, the oldest a rosy-cheeked fellow who could have been seventy or more; the youngest a pair of twelve year olds. The boys were hired to play the female roles. Any other arrangements, involving the use of unchaperoned girls or women, would have been unseemly.

Hamlet stood in the shadows for a few minutes, watching with affection, before the manager of the little company saw him and came to him with hands outstretched and words pouring from his mouth.

Hamlet smiled and shook both his hands. 'You are welcome, masters, welcome all. I am glad to see you. Welcome, good friends.' He moved among them, shaking more hands. 'My old friend, your face is fringed since I saw you last. Now you have bearded me in my own lair. Ah, young Felix, you will not be playing the role of a lady much longer if you keep growing at this rate. My word, your voice will soon betray you. Claudio, you have not aged a whit. Braybar, what a fine Romeo you were. What entertainment have you brought us, good sirs?'

'We plan to perform *The Murder of Gonzago*, God willing, and may it please Your Royal Highness.'

'Ah! Most suitable. You've brought it to the right place.' Hamlet caught sight of Polonius scurrying through the hall on one of his errands. Polonius always looked as though he were on the way from some-where important to somewhere even more important. But Hamlet, in a tone he did not often use, arrested the old man just as he was about to vanish down a corner corridor. 'Polonius! I need you.'

Polonius swerved and trotted straight to the prince without missing a beat. 'Highness, I am ever at your service.'

'Then kindly find some lodgings for these fine fellows. Be generous to them, for they are the ones who tell the stories of our times. Never mind getting a good epitaph after you're dead if you got a bad report from this lot while you're still alive.'

'Highness, I will arrange their accommodation,

though it is not part of my normal duties. It really falls within the province of the comptroller of the household. But I will treat them as they deserve, depend upon it.'

'As they deserve! You will have to do better than that! Treat every man as he deserves and no one'll escape a whipping. Treat them with as much honour and dignity as you'd treat yourself, Polonius. If you treat a man better than he deserves, why then the more admirable your generosity.'

Polonius, not quite so unruffled now, bowed and nodded to the actors to follow him. But Hamlet held back the manager, waiting until the others had gathered their bits and pieces and shuffled off after Polonius. An idea had come to him while he was organising their welcome to Elsinore. 'Tell me, my friend,' he said, when they were alone together. 'You mentioned *The Murder of Gonzago*.'

'I did Highness, but we can do *Romeo and Juliet* if that is your wish. It's not a bad bit of work, although a bit far-fetched. Or we have a new comedy, a satiric piece, rather short, but most diverting, judging by the reactions we got in the south, where we…'

'No, no, *The Murder of Gonzago* is an excellent choice. But tell me, if I wrote a speech of some dozen or sixteen lines, you could learn that and insert it in the play, could you not?'

Rather startled, the actor was nevertheless good enough at his craft to show no emotion. 'Certainly, if that is what Your Highness wishes.'

'Good. Then, for now, follow the others. Mention nothing of this to the old man, Polonius. I'll write the speech and deliver it to you by dinner time. We can have the play tomorrow night.'

'Very good, Your Royal Highness.'

And off he went, leaving the prince with his thoughts. They tumbled around in his mind, busy as a line of laundry in a windstorm. 'What can I say for myself?' he wondered. 'I, who have done nothing? What can I say in my defence? I have seen these actors stand upon a stage and make themselves weep over the dead children of Hecuba. Real tears come out of their eyes! Hecuba, who lived, if she lived at all, two thousand years ago! Hecuba, who was turned into a dog and drowned. What's Hecuba to them or they to Hecuba? Yet the tears run down their faces as they ponder her fate! If they can do that in a play, what would they do if they had real cause for passion? What would any of them do?

'By God, if they were in my situation they would

weep. They would drown the stage with tears and burn the audience with the fire of their words. They would make the guilty mad, and appal the innocent. The eyes and ears of the spectators would fill to overflowing. And yet, here I am, and what do I do? Why, that's easy? I play games with a racquet and a ball. A king has his kingdom and his life stolen away, and I am silent. My father is murdered and I sit down to table with his murderer. What does that make me? A coward, nothing else. One who has the liver of a pigeon.

'If I were anything else, if I had a heart, and the guts to match it, I would have scattered the insides of this treacherous king across the fields to fatten the crows. That traitor. That bastard. That bloody bawdy villain, remorseless, treacherous, lecherous and vile. And all I can do, with my father come from heaven and hell or somewhere in between, telling me to take revenge, is to wallow in words. Muttering and cursing and bellowing.

'Well, at least I have a plan now. I have heard that guilty creatures faced with a re-enactment of their crime fall on their knees and confess. I'll have these actors play something like the murder of my father in front of my uncle tomorrow night. I'll watch him, I'll study him, and if he so much as blanches or trembles I'll know the truth and I'll know my course of action.

'After all, I still cannot be certain what I saw that night. Was it my father? Did it tell me the truth? Or was it some fiend sent to lie and confuse and do evil? The devil can take any shape he wants, including that of my father. And while I am so sad about his passing, the devil has the perfect chance to take advantage of me.

'That is what holds me back. It is a terrible thing to be a coward but it is not so bad to be prudent. Well, tomorrow shall tell the next chapter of my story.

'The play's the thing, wherein I'll test the conscience of the king!'

FIFTEEN

The performance started late. The servants were supposed to take out all the tables from the state dining hall after dinner, but the head butler said it was nothing to do with him, furniture-moving wasn't his job, his responsibilities ended with clearing the meal, and apparently no one had told the comptroller of the royal household, who was in charge of entertainment, and the deputy housekeeper, who looked after the reception rooms, was laid up with pleurisy, so in the end Hamlet and a couple of guards and the manager of the troupe did it themselves.

By the time the chairs were arranged and two

curtains hung it was ten o'clock.

Outside the wind had become blustery, with gusts of real wildness. The Danish flag was nearly ripped from its pole on the western tenement and tiles were blown from the castle roof. There were some who did not bother to return to the dining hall but stayed in their rooms with a bottle of wine, or a pack of cards, or a few friends for a gossip. Afterwards, when they heard, they regretted their inertia.

The actors were brought in from the anteroom which had been assigned them for dressing. Hamlet had been furious as he moved tables and chairs but now anxiety was his dominant emotion again. The actors became aware of his tension when he started to coach them in their craft. Much as they liked him and appreciated his patronage, they were not necessarily keen to have him tell them how to do their jobs. But he was a prince and they were commoners; indeed in many places they were treated as little better than beggars or riffraff. Hamlet was almost alone among the nobility of Denmark in his respect for them.

'Do the speech as I taught it to you,' he urged them. 'For that matter, do all the speeches with expression. If you just rattle off your lines like you're reciting a list of groceries, as I've seen some actors do, I might as well fetch the cooks from the kitchen to read them. And don't be extravagant. The more passionate the scene, the more subtle should be your gestures. The contrast between the whirlwind of passion and the moderation of gesture is what gives a scene its smoothness. How I hate to hear some fellow on a stage ranting and raving! Let the words do the work. You need not bellow like a cow giving birth, or stride up and down in a frenzy. I would have an actor like that whipped for trying to out-Thor the god of thunder himself!'

'Yes, Your Royal Highness,' one of the actors said.

Hamlet hesitated at the man's tone. 'I was only joking about the whipping.'

'Yes, Highness.'

Hamlet shook his head. 'Suit the action to the words and the words to the action. Your task is to hold up a mirror to nature. If you give a scene more tragedy than nature has given it, or more sentimentality, or more drama, you have ruined it. I have seen actors, even famous ones, who in imitating men or women do such a poor job that I started to wonder whether they were in fact human, or perhaps some lower form of life created not by nature but by one of nature's incompetent assistants.'

'I hope we do a little better than that, Highness,' said the leader of the troupe.

'Do a lot better! A whole lot better! And, by the way, whoever plays the clown, make sure not to laugh at your own jokes! There are always a few fools in the audience who find that amusing, but when such an actor steals the scene, important lines are lost. It shows pitiful ambition on his part. Anyway, enough, go behind the curtains, make yourselves ready.'

They trickled away. As they went out to the right Horatio came in from the left. Hamlet was warmed to see him. 'Horatio, dear Horatio, the most just man I ever met.'

'Hamlet, no,' Horatio protested.

'Oh I'm not flattering you. What would be the point? You don't have any wealth, except your good spirits, to feed and clothe you. But I tell you this, Horatio, since I was old enough to judge between the people of my acquaintance, you are the one to whom I've always turned. I respect the way you've handled the good things that come to you as much as the way you've dealt with adversity. Blessed are those who have good judgment! Blessed are those who do not allow fortune to play them like they are a trumpet, letting her decide what notes she will sound! Give me the man who is not a slave to passion and he will be the blood of my heart, as you are mine, Horatio.'

Horatio blushed with pleasure. His affection for Hamlet was deep and genuine, but much as they met on terms as equal as could be found between prince and commoner, Horatio had been aware from earliest childhood of the uncrossable social gulf between them. He could not help being flattered to be told that he was the closest to the popular and beautiful prince, the man who would one day be king.

With a hand around Horatio's shoulder Hamlet walked him to the other end of the room. He spoke more confidentially. 'Now, pay close attention. In a few minutes the actors will begin the play. There is a scene set in an orchard, and it portrays the murder of a king. I want you, when it comes to that scene, to study my uncle closely. Watch him with the eyes of your soul. I tell you this, Horatio, the ghost who visited me on that dreadful night brought me a story which may have come from the devil, as we speculated, for he told of a devilish act. I hope to find out some truth tonight. When my uncle sees the actors on stage he may be looking at a mirror to the past. That is what we have to establish.'

'Hamlet, I tremble to hear your words. You seem

to be hinting at the unthinkable.'

'You must think the unthinkable, old friend, as I have done since that night on the terrace.'

So, there it was again, the reference to the event which was still veiled from Horatio. He stood, deeply troubled, and lost in thought. At heart he knew he had no choice but to do as his friend and royal master asked, but he feared the consequences. After a moment he gave Hamlet a little smile.

'Very well, I will do as you say. I will watch the king so closely that if he steals anything during the play and I don't see it, I'll pay for whatever he stole.'

'Well said, good friend. Treasonous, but witty. Quick, they are coming. To your place.'

Polonius led Claudius and Gertrude into the room, making sure all was ready for them. Ophelia followed close behind. The king was full of beer and cheer, beaming at Hamlet. 'How is our nephew and our son?' he asked.

'Why, I forgot to ask them, last time I saw them,' Hamlet said. 'But I believe they would say that they were well, though perhaps a little empty from eating air stuffed with promises.'

The king, determined not to be annoyed, smiled briefly, without humour. 'I have nothing to do with that answer, Hamlet,' he said. 'Those words are not for me; they are not mine.'

'No, nor mine either, now,' Hamlet said. 'They have left my body and my mouth and are gone. It may be that they have no owner at all.' He put his head around the side of the makeshift curtain and whispered into the darkness. 'Are you ready?'

'Yes, Your Royal Highness.'

'Very good. Remember all that I told you.'

'We will, Your Royal Highness.'

Hamlet faced the audience again. At least sixty people from around the castle had gathered for the show. Mostly lords and ladies-in-waiting, the king's cronies and Gertrude's confidantes, old Voltimand, who had once been chancellor, Polonius with his children, Laertes and Ophelia, the inseparable Rosencrantz and Guildenstern, Reynaldo, their Majesties' secretaries and other high-placed court officials, a few army officers—most of them seemed uninterested, some were probably drunk, and a couple were undoubtedly deaf.

In a corner at the back of the room, in darkness, stood those of the domestic staff who wished to attend: footmen, maids, kitchen hands, even a couple of young gardeners. Garath, their overseer, had let them go, but it was against his better judgment. To him, those who worked outside should stay outside, and those who worked inside could stay inside and get on with their games.

Ophelia sat in the front row. Behind her, leering over her shoulder, was Osric, the lean young farmer, his tall frame pinched into a tight wooden chair. He was laughing immoderately at some quip of Claudius's. 'That's rich, Your Majesty,' he called out. 'Oh that's very rich.'

'Too much cider,' Hamlet thought. He gathered himself up. 'Ladies and gentlemen, the play is about to begin. The name—well, I am calling it *The Mousetrap*. But don't take that too literally. It is the story of a murder done in Vienna. Gonzago is the name of the duke, and his wife is Baptista. It's a nasty story, but what if it is? It won't affect us. Let the pained horse cringe when the saddle goes on him again: we are still unridden. We are all innocents here. Now be silent, please, so that these good fellows who have come so far can entertain us.'

He led the audience in a meagre round of clapping, which petered out as soon as Hamlet stopped.

'Come and sit by me, Hamlet,' Gertrude called.

'No, mother, here's a more attractive bush where a man can pitch his tent.' One of the servant girls giggled immoderately from the dark rear of the room, and got a quick smack from a housekeeper. Hamlet strode to where Ophelia sat. He ignored the empty seat on her left and instead crouched beside her. 'May I put myself between your legs?' he whispered.

The beautiful girl blushed. 'No, my lord.'

'I meant, to sit on the floor here, in front of you.'

'No, my lord.'

Polonius leaned across and muttered to the king, 'He's in love with her all right.'

But neither of the young people heard him. Hamlet was too engrossed in flirting with Ophelia. 'When I talked about pitching a tent,' he asked her teasingly, 'did you think I meant in the country?'

She either did not understand or refused to play the game. 'I thought nothing, my lord.'

Hamlet sighed theatrically. 'And going between your legs, what did you think I had in mind?'

'Again, I say nothing, my lord.'

'You are right. And it's a pretty piece of scenery to have between a maiden's legs.'

'What is, my lord?'

'Nothing. Though there are some things I would not like to find. Indeed, a nothing can be a something, and the nothing something can be sweet indeed.

As can the something nothing. But the something something—ah, I could tell you a story I heard of Rosencrantz in Copenhagen, and how one night he found a something something where he expected to find a something nothing.'

Ophelia could not help giggling, earning a glare from Polonius and a 'sshh' from Gertrude. While the two young people were whispering the play had begun, but so far all was in mime. Now a new actor took the stage and launched into a long speech which quickly bored both Hamlet and Ophelia. They resumed their surreptitious conversation.

'You are in a good mood tonight, my lord,' murmured Ophelia.

'What should I do but be merry? Look at my mother, and her cheerful face. And it's only two hours since my father died. Obviously there's no reason for anyone to be sad about anything.'

'Oh no! It has been a long time since the king died, my lord.'

'A long time? A long time, you say? Well then, let the devil wear the black, for I'll get out my party clothes. A long time! And not forgotten yet! There must be hope that the memory of a great man may outlive him by a few years then. If he's so greedy that he wants more, then he'd better build a pyramid and put his name on it.'

'Sssssssshhhhhhhh,' hissed the queen.

Hamlet lapsed into silence again, leaning against Ophelia.

He always comes back to the same obsessions, she thought. Why can't he let it go? Why can't he just enjoy life?

SEVENTEEN

By the time Ophelia could work out the story of the play it was well advanced, although she soon decided it was too wordy. Ophelia's intelligence was that of instinct and emotion; Hamlet's was of books and science. The actor playing a king who has been married to his queen a long time tells her that he feels his life will soon be over. He starts to speak of the husband who will replace him when he is gone. At this point the queen becomes violently emotional and swears that she won't be marrying anybody else. She strides around the stage waving her arms and declaiming, so quickly that it is hard to understand the words.

Ophelia yawned. Whatever the boy playing the queen was using for bosoms was not working very well; they were slipping down his front. Ophelia looked at Hamlet. The light from the fireplace reflecting from his white hair made it shine like the halos of the holy family in the paintings. Was that sacrilege, she wondered, to compare Hamlet to Christ? Would it be too flirtatious of her to stroke his hair? She knew what her father would say. Polonius would already be furious at the way they were sitting. She could expect a stinging lecture tonight, and banishment to her room for a few days probably, as well. Why couldn't he understand how she felt? Why did he have to be so horrible and strict…Not like other girls' fathers.

Ophelia decided she had better not run her hand through Hamlet's hair. Not yet anyway. A glance from the tiniest corner of her eye gave her the sense that Polonius was watching. She dared not look at him directly. Instead, she turned her attention back to the stage.

There the queen was still proclaiming her love for her husband. 'I would kill my husband a second time,' she vowed, 'were I to marry someone else after you have gone. Earth shall not feed me, nor heaven give me light, games shall not amuse me, nor sleep give me rest, if I bestow my attention on anyone but you. I would rather live as a hermit in a cave than be with another man.'

Ophelia whispered to Hamlet, 'She takes a long time to say she loves him.'

'A woman's love lasts no longer than her words,' he whispered.

She sat back, angry. Is that all he thought of women then? Would he treat her love as mere trash? Did he not understand the power of the lifelong gift she had for him?

The young boy playing the role of the queen finally came to a halt. He stood in the centre of the stage and announced, with an impressively deep voice, 'Let my life be nothing but strife, if once a widow, I become a wife!'

His bosom had settled at a point just above his navel.

Hamlet, whom Ophelia decided may have had too much beer, called out to the queen, 'What do you think, mother?'

'What do I think? I think the more people talk about love the less they feel it.'

But suddenly Claudius was interrupting both

them and the play. 'Is this thing some sort of insult to her majesty and me?' he demanded.

Ophelia stiffened, wishing then that she had paid more attention to the discussion on stage.

Gamely the actors struggled on, as Hamlet replied to his uncle, 'No, no, it's all a joke. Relax, sir. There's no offence in the world.'

On stage the king was 'asleep' on a grassy bank, a rather unreliable-looking prop covered with a green blanket and a scattering of flowers. Prowling around him was a new character. No sooner did Ophelia wonder who he was than Hamlet whispered, 'That's Lucianus, nephew to the king.'

Ophelia whispered back, 'You make a good commentator, my lord.'

The nephew came to the front of the stage. Ophelia felt the excitement quivering through Hamlet. She wondered at the cause. Could it be her? What strange creatures men were. What powerful passions they seemed to feel. She felt intense passions too, but men seemed hot and cold, whereas she was always hot. It never occurred to her that Hamlet was trembling with the tension of a first-time author who is about to hear his lines uttered in front of an audience.

Glaring first at the audience and then at the recumbent king, the nephew made his evil intentions clear.

> There he sleeps, in mortal bliss,
> but I am like a serpent's hiss.
> I carry here venom profound,
> gathered from this very ground.
> Infected by my evil vice,
> every bite will poison twice.
> Pour it into this one here,
> through the medium of his ear!
> End at last his virtuous life,
> so I can carry off...

Before the actor was able to carry out his attack on the sleeping king, Hamlet leapt to his feet in wild excitement. 'He poisons him in the garden to get the estate! He poisoned him I tell you. He poured it in his ear! He murdered him in the garden, murdered him, and stole his wife. Stole everything he owned.'

'Is he drunk or mad?' Ophelia wondered, frightened. She did not understand what was happening, but she felt the ferocity of the moment. Leaning forward, she saw the king stirring to his feet. She whispered to Hamlet, 'My lord, I think the king is offended'

'Stop the play!' Claudius shouted, trembling with rage and fear.

'What?' Hamlet exulted. 'Frightened by false fire? It's only a play, after all.'

Behind Ophelia, Osric struggled to get out of his seat. 'Shame, shame,' he brayed.

Gertrude was standing. 'Are you all right, my lord?' she begged her husband.

'Stop the play,' Polonius called.

All was confusion. The actors had already melted back behind the curtains, where their manager was cursing Hamlet. 'He's dropped us right in it,' he muttered. 'Hurry back and pack your bags, lads. Pack everything. We might have to do a fast exit.'

'Give me some light,' roared the king. 'Fetch a light.'

'Lights, lights,' Polonius called, to no one in particular. A candle was brought from the rear of the hall, and more candles were lit from it. The king was stumbling about like a wounded bear. He walked right over Osric who had fallen forwards, narrowly missing Ophelia, and was lying face down on the floor. 'Shame shame!' he called again, feeling the king's heavy boot in his back. Then he vomited.

Claudius could now see a clear path to the door.

The servants, trying to flee, had to stand back; they bowed low as he passed, hoping he would not see their faces. The two young gardeners were scared out of their wits. They both had the same thought: 'Old Garath was right. Should have listened to old Garath. He knows a thing or two, that one.'

Claudius was out the door. Hamlet, listening, heard the clatter of his heavy boots on the staircase. The king was followed closely by Gertrude, then Polonius, who forgot his daughter in his haste to catch up with the king. Ophelia hovered for a minute, her eyes fixed on Hamlet, before she too fled. The others took their cue, and made hurried departures. Though no one understood what had happened, there was a strong feeling that it would be best to lie low and stay away. So off they scurried. In a remarkably short time Hamlet and Horatio were left alone.

EIGHTEEN

There was complete silence behind the curtain. 'Well, well,' Hamlet gloated. 'Do you think I could get a job writing for actors, if all else goes sour for me?'

'Half a job perhaps,' said Horatio.

'Oh a full one, I think. I wrote that whole speech about the serpent. And it got a better reaction than the rest of the play put together.'

'It didn't make sense,' Horatio objected. 'How is a serpent supposed to gather venom from the ground?'

'Don't be so literal. It's poetry. It isn't supposed to make sense. But oh, Horatio, did you see the king's face?'

'I did indeed.'

'The ghost knew what he was talking about, all right. Did you see Claudius's reaction to the talk of poisoning?'

'I did, though I wish I could say I did not.'

'Now my path becomes clearer. But hello, who's this? Why a couple of good fellows. Rosencrantz and Guildenstern, if I'm not mistaken. Come, a pair of fiddlers, are you not? Let's have some music from you.'

The two courtiers, both of whom had become rather stout in recent times, looked hot and flustered. Hamlet's greeting threw them into an even worse state. 'Your Royal Highness, we are not fiddlers,' Rosencrantz began.

'No indeed,' Guildenstern agreed. 'The king, sir, the king…'

'Yes, what of the king? Let us hear news of the king.'

Hamlet was still in a wild state. Horatio, who had once seen an overexcited colt run into a fence and kill himself, wanted to calm him before he did something truly dangerous. Committed an act that could not be recalled. No act can be recalled but Hamlet looked ready to precipitate a landslide, without a thought as to who might be buried in its path.

'Good sir, let me have a word with you,' Rosencrantz tried again.

'Not only a word, my dear fellow, you can have an entire book. And you may pick the topic.'

Rosencrantz and Guildenstern glanced at each other. Their lips flickered in a silent signal: 'He's hopeless—what can be done with him?'

Hamlet did not notice, but loyal Horatio did.

'The king is in the throne room,' Rosencrantz said, 'and is much distempered.'

'With drink?' asked Hamlet.

'Sir!' Guildenstern took a step backwards.

'No, no, his blood pressure…he is in a fit,' Rosencrantz said.

'That sounds serious. Roll him on his side and make sure he does not swallow his tongue. I would do it myself but he might misunderstand my intentions.'

Guildenstern tried a different tack. 'And the queen, sir, your mother…'

'Yes, she is. Thank you for letting me know.'

'Your Royal Highness, please, could you allow us to deliver our message. It is very difficult when Your Highness speaks in this manner.'

'I will tame myself. Commence.'

Both men took deep breaths and looked at each

other again. It seemed to be decided that Rosencrantz would begin.

'The queen, in great affliction of spirit, has sent us to you…'

'And you are welcome.'

But now Guildenstern had had enough. Normally the quieter of the two, he felt he had lost enough dignity in front of Horatio, and so stood upon the little he had left. 'Your Royal Highness,' he said coldly, 'you tell us we are welcome, but your courtesy is not of the right breed. If it pleases you to make us a straightforward answer we will carry out your mother's wishes; if not, you must give us permission to withdraw and that will be the end of our business.'

To the surprise of everyone, Hamlet answered calmly, in the lilting voice he used to chat to servants about their babies, or diplomats about their hats. 'Gentlemen, I cannot.'

'What, sir?' Guildenstern stammered.

Horatio, for some reason that he did not understand himself, felt a sudden surge of care for Hamlet. He eased a little closer to the prince.

'I cannot give you a plain answer. My mind is diseased. I am ill. However, I will answer you as best I can, so go ahead—if you have a message from my mother, as you seem to, then deliver it.'

'Then, sir,' Rosencrantz said nervously. 'She says that your behaviour amazes and astonishes her.'

'Oh, wonderful son, who can astonish a mother. But is there a sequel to this? I can hardly believe you have come here to tell me just that.'

It was Guildenstern's turn again. 'She would like to see you in her apartment before you go to bed.'

'She is not likely to see me in her apartment after I go to bed. That would be a strange state of affairs.' Hamlet had danced away again, back to the edge of the precipice. 'But palace life these days is nothing but strange affairs. Something is rotten in the state of Denmark.'

Rosencrantz and Guildenstern looked aghast, fearing they were about to hear terrible words that would make them partners in some sort of conspiracy. 'I beg you, Your Royal Highness,' they said in perfect harmony.

'Well, that makes it unanimous,' Hamlet said. 'Anyway I would obey any summons from the queen, even if she were only one-tenth of the mother she is. Have you any further business with me?'

'Highness,' said Rosencrantz, wheedling now. He

reached out a hand as if to take the prince by the shoulder. 'You loved me once.'

'And still do,' said Hamlet, unflinching.

'Then, please, why do you behave like this? You have been lost to your friends, to those who love you. Where is the sweet prince who was once such a merry companion?'

You didn't know him too well, Horatio thought.

And Hamlet had an almost identical reaction: if that's all they knew of me, they knew little indeed.

'Gentlemen,' he said, 'I lack prospects.'

'But you will inherit one day! The king has always spoken of you as the one who will replace him. How can you say you lack prospects?'

Hamlet shrugged. 'Among the growing grass the horse can still starve.' He picked up a flute and handed it to Guildenstern. 'Play this for me,' he said.

'Highness,' said Guildenstern, putting his hands behind his back, 'I cannot.'

'Please?'

'Sir, I can't!'

'I beg you.'

'It is not possible, Your Highness, believe me. I don't know how!'

'Go on.'

'I wouldn't know where to start. I have never learned music.'

'Oh, you're making too much fuss. There's nothing to it. It's as easy as lying. Use your fingers and thumb to cover these holes—give it breath with your mouth and it will make the most beautiful music. Look, here are the stops.'

'But I can make no harmony. I don't have the skill.'

'Why, then, look at what you are doing to me. You would play upon me as though I am a flute, you think you know my stops, you would sound me from the lowest notes to the highest…yet here is this little flute, which contains much excellent music, and which you cannot make speak. By God, do you think I am easier to be played on than a pipe? Call me what instrument you will, try as you might to reach my heart, you cannot play upon me, sir!'

Both Rosencrantz and Guildenstern were unable to respond. As they looked at each other in consternation Polonius appeared silently behind them. He seemed to have shrunk in the space of an evening. Hamlet had always thought of him as old but now he looked ninety. Huddled into his robes with just his dry wrinkled little head protruding, he called to Hamlet. 'Highness, the queen would like to speak to you, as soon as possible.'

Hamlet stared at him. 'Do you see the cloud through the window there?' he asked. 'The one which looks like a camel?'

Polonius made a pretence of looking through the window. Outside was black as a grave. 'Indeed, it is like a camel,' he said.

'Actually, I think it's like a rabbit.'

'Yes, now that you mention it, it does have the shape of a rabbit.'

'Or a whale?' Hamlet asked.

'Very like a whale.'

'Then I will come to my mother in the next ten minutes.'

'I will tell her, Your Royal Highness.'

Polonius withdrew. Rosencrantz and Guildenstern took advantage of the moment to go with him. Hamlet nodded to Horatio who gave a slight bow and followed the others.

Hamlet was left alone, his mind still whirling with the excitement of the evening, and the success of his plot. He felt that events were now about to accelerate towards a terrible climax. Gazing out the same window that Polonius had glanced at, he noticed the extreme darkness. The wind was still pulling at the building and rattling the shutters. 'It's the witching time of night,' he thought. 'When graves yawn open and hell itself exhales diseases and decay. Now is my opportunity. Now I could commit bitter acts, of a kind that daylight would fear to look upon. Now my sword can become a serpent. Now I could drink hot blood. But first, I will go to my mother.'

He drew a deep breath and straightened up.

'Oh heart,' he told himself, 'do not lose your nature. Let me not be evil, think evil, or act from evil thoughts. I will say what I want to say to my mother but I will do nothing violent towards her. With her, my tongue and my soul shall contradict each other. I will speak daggers to her but use none. However much I shame her with words, I shall do nothing shameful to her.'

He left the room.

NINETEEN

There had been a day in their childhood when Ophelia saw the timidity of Hamlet. It was in April, the weakest month. He picked up Horatio and Ophelia one morning, when the two boys were nearly twelve and Ophelia nearly eleven, and led them from the southern wing back to his tower, down the final steps and out of the castle. They ran through the western gate, yelling cheek at the young Dutch guard, whom they liked, and on into the village.

Hamlet went this way often enough. The people here admired him and stopped what they were doing when they saw him coming, left their work, moving forward eagerly. Some clapped, a few girls called his name, half a dozen boys ran down the hill after the young prince and his friends.

Hamlet, however, paused for nothing or no one until they were in the forest. By then Horatio was nearly fifty metres behind and Ophelia was white in the distance, a goose perhaps, a bird struggling for her life.

Hamlet stopped and watched her. He seemed fascinated with her today.

'What are we doing?' Ophelia asked, when she caught up to them and had finished panting.

'I don't know. Looking for the monster? Searching for dragons? I felt possessed by the running urge.'

Horatio looked cross. 'I thought we were doing something special.'

Hamlet ignored him and smiled at Ophelia. 'We are. Maybe. Who knows?'

They walked on, calm now, chatting only of the here and now, the faint track to the left, the spider scuttling across their path, the piece of bark patterned like the king's personal standard.

'Do you know this road?' Horatio asked the prince.

'No. But I imagine it leads to Eligah.'

'I went there when I was little, with my father. But I don't think we came this way. Anyway, we were in a carriage. I wasn't paying much attention.'

'What's Eligah?' asked Ophelia from behind them.

'A village. They make cheese, mostly. Haven't you heard of Eligah cheese?'

She didn't answer.

A thumping from the left hinted at a wild boar and the three children walked closer together, looking eagerly and anxiously from side to side. Only a few weeks earlier a baby had been taken by a boar, or so it was believed, and the villagers were still trying to hunt the beast down. But the forest was quiet and the road clear.

Soon it became monotonous, and Horatio, who liked everything to have meaning and purpose, almost suggested turning back. But a glance at Hamlet's face dissuaded him. The young prince was intent on something. He looked more like a jungle hunter than a boy travelling through the woods in Denmark.

They walked for nearly two hours and reached the outskirts of Eligah. Now Horatio became more interested. Here was an interruption, here was the quickness that comes only with people. The village was larger than he remembered, with an ancient bridge just ahead of them, and a tall church spire in the distance. On both sides of the track were pig and dairy farms, the tiniest farms Horatio had ever seen. He began to wonder if he had ever been here at all.

To his frustration, however, Hamlet stopped.

'Time we were heading back,' he announced.

'But why have we come all this way?' Horatio objected. Already he was sulking, knowing that his wishes would not prevail. It was not just that Hamlet was a prince; it was also that Horatio was not quite strong enough.

'How would you like it,' Ophelia said shrewdly, 'if you couldn't go anywhere without people making a fuss of you? He's entitled to some privacy.'

'But you don't know if that's what he's thinking,' Horatio said.

'Don't talk about him as if he's not here.'

'Well, that's exactly what you were just doing.'

Hamlet watched the squabble with interest, smiling slightly. He had nothing more to say, though, and started walking back along the clear wide track. Horatio was baffled. Why had they come here? Had there been no reason after all?

At that moment there was a cry from Hamlet's

left and slightly behind him. Horatio and Ophelia stood frozen, listening and staring. Hamlet seemed to need no time to study the situation. At the first sound he was already running and in a moment had passed them.

He has the reflexes of a dog, Horatio thought, grudgingly, admiringly, enviously. Then he followed his prince.

Hamlet had dashed through a screen of trees as though they were not there, and was already out of sight. When Horatio burst through the same line of young elms he saw Hamlet stooping over a dark shape on the ground. Horatio first thought this was the baby taken by the boar but then realised that was not possible; the baby had disappeared three weeks ago.

There seemed to be no danger. The boy ran to Hamlet's side and stood with him looking down at the creature. It was not a baby but a badger, wounded in some wild attack, by a wolf perhaps. Its snout had been half torn off its face. It was an old badger, with a greying muzzle, as much as could be seen of it through the blood. Its teeth, exposed in its distress, were worn and stained.

With the arrival of Horatio, and then Ophelia, the badger stirred and tried to drag itself away, on three wobbly legs, the fourth trailing behind, so impotent that for a moment Horatio thought it was a stick the badger had caught in its fur. The creature struggled about ten metres and collapsed again. It lay there waiting in fear for the end. Until then death had meant nothing more than the avoidance of pain; now the creature understood oblivion.

'Better finish him off,' Horatio said to Hamlet.

The prince drew his sword, a short weapon, as befitted boys of their age, but sharp enough. The three of them had followed the badger and now they stood over it once more, watching its heaving flanks and tiny eyes, listening to its grunting breath.

'Do it,' Ophelia said urgently. 'I can't stand it. Poor thing.'

Hamlet held the handle of his sword. He had not yet fully withdrawn it from its scabbard. Horatio realised that he was hesitating, that perhaps he was not yet ready to use it. Some boys were like that, but he'd never imagined Hamlet might be one of them. He didn't know what to say but thought he should say something. Wisely, though, he held his tongue.

'Go on,' Ophelia said again. 'It's all right. It's the only thing to do. Look at its face. It can't survive.'

'I…' Hamlet said. 'I don't think it's big enough.'

'Of course it is,' Ophelia said. She had not yet understood the problem. Hamlet could not do it in front of anyone, only on his own. 'Please Hamlet. The pain it is…you must put it out of its misery. Nothing in such pain should live.'

Hamlet jerked and swallowed. 'You…I can't…' he said. 'Why should I? Oh all right then.' And he stabbed angrily at the badger, missing the heart by such a margin that the sword went in somewhere along the back of the spine, near the tail. The badger grunted and flailed its legs. Hamlet realised the enormity of his mistake and stabbed wildly now, three, four times, until blood was everywhere across the ground and breath was leaving the spasming animal.

For every breath the badger lost Hamlet breathed harder, and now that the creature had nothing left the boy panted, as if somehow breathing for them both. Soon, it was over. In anger and embarrassment he looked around for his two friends. They had backed away and were behind him now, Ophelia with averted eyes, Horatio frowning.

'It's different with bow and arrow,' Hamlet said. His anger felt like scarlet fever. If I were here on my own I would stab myself, he thought. That would be easy. But I wouldn't do it in front of anyone. I'd probably mess that up too.

The best swordsman in the castle, for his age! Horatio was thinking. Probably the best in the country! But he went to water. I would have done it with one clean stroke. I'll be better than him one day.

And as they walked home in silence, Horatio trailing behind the other two, he practised huge stabbing strokes at the prince's back, realising with terror as he did that such a thing was tantamount to treason.

TWENTY

Claudius, Rosencrantz and Guildenstern met in the library moments after the play finished. The king strode up and down the room, past the heavy ranks of books that muffled all sound, pulling at his beard, wild-eyed and sweating. 'I just don't like him,' he said. 'I don't care whether he's disturbed in his mind or what his problem is. I'm not going to have him rampaging around the place like a madman. He'll have to go away for a while. Under escort. And you can take him. Yes, that's it. You two shall take him somewhere, shall shepherd him.'

Rosencrantz nodded solemnly. 'Your Majesty, in a

family the father influences his wife and his children and those others who live in the house. But in the family of a whole country, millions of people rely upon your good government. Whatever it takes to help the security of Denmark, depend on us to do it.'

'Truly, when a king sighs,' Guildenstern joined in, 'the whole nation groans. Any person must have an effect on himself and others, but the impact of a king is magnified a multitude of times.'

There was a time when Claudius dreamed of hearing such things, when he had imagined that the flattery of courtiers would be sweet to the ears and like roses to the nose. But in the heat generated by Hamlet's trick with the play he had no patience with such talk. He snapped his fingers at the two men and nodded dismissal, just as Polonius bustled in through the little doorway beside the fireplace.

'Majesty,' he said, pink-faced with the excitement of a new plot. 'Majesty,' he repeated, 'he's on his way to his mother's suite.'

No need to say who 'he' was. Hamlet dominated Elsinore tonight, as so often before, even during times when he hadn't done much. This night, with an attack on the king that could hardly have been more direct, he strode the castle stage with unassailable power.

'I'll hide myself behind the screen to hear what's going on,' Polonius volunteered. 'As you said to me just the other day, and no disrespect to her majesty of course, sometimes it's wise not to rely on a mother's account. It is natural for her to be biased, and therefore best for an independent witness to be present.'

Claudius betrayed his wife without a second thought. It was just another business matter, another precaution, one more hole in the fence to be checked. All measures were justified if Hamlet were planning a coup. 'Good, very good, my friend, tell me everything. I have just arranged with Rosencrantz and Guildenstern to take Hamlet away somewhere. They will escort him and keep him safe—and, by the way, keep me safe at the same time. Now make haste.'

The old man, glowing with the righteousness that only the rudest know, hurried away to his self-appointed task.

Now at last the king was left alone. It was not common for him to be alone these days. He stood still for a full minute after Polonius closed the door. Then, unexpectedly, he sank to his knees. He was even surprised at himself. He was always strong in front of others, but suddenly there was no mask to be kept in place. Take away the mask and what is left? Take away the façade of a building and the interior is exposed. And sometimes the building is empty.

A deep sob arose in him and he realised he would not be able to hold it back. It was like a huge bubble in a hot mud pool, coming to the surface and flowering in black. 'Oh!' he half grunted, half groaned, as it burst from his mouth. 'Oh! My crime is foul. It smells to the highest heaven. A brother's murder. The earliest of crimes, the worst of crimes. Cain killed Abel and I have followed in his path. I want to pray! I feel such a desire to pray. Yet I cannot. Forgiveness might be mine, if I could pray. The whitening rain of heaven might fall upon me and wash me clean. But I can't find the words. "Forgive the awful crime I have committed?" How can I say that when I am in possession of all that I gained from my bloody deed? My crown, my queen, and the life I coveted. Can one be pardoned yet still retain the profits? On earth, yes, perhaps, maybe, with a word here and a payment there, but in heaven, no. There the sight is keen and the understanding perfect. What is there to hope for?'

The long lines of leather-bound books looked down on him impassively. Behind Claudius came Hamlet, on his way to his mother, but entering the library in search of a lavatory. By the dying light of the coals in the fireplace, surrounded by shelves of bibles and religious commentaries, he saw a dark shape crouched on the moth-holed carpet. He crept forwards and was transfixed to see his enemy delivered up to him, kneeling with his back turned, like a target at the archers range. He was mumbling away to himself but Hamlet could not make out the words above the scream of the wind at the windows. The prince stood in an ecstasy of shock. This was the very thing he wanted, the moment he had longed for. If ever a time offered itself up to be seized this was it. King on a plate, and Hamlet had the cutlery. His hand flew to the hilt of his sword. For so long now he had lain awake or walked the castle's ramparts with his hand on that sword, dreaming of killing the monster. The uproar at the play had brought matters to a head. Blood must be spilt.

Now I can do it, Hamlet exulted. Now he is mine. Revenge is mine. He was creeping forwards even as his mind formed the thoughts. He knew his sword would make a sound as he withdrew it from its scabbard, therefore he resolved not to draw it until he was within a few steps of the praying king. It would be done with perfect speed. The king, mumbling prayers that Hamlet could not hear, was lost in his devotions and so he would lose his life.

Yet suddenly an awful thought gripped the young prince. Prayers! Praying! What was he thinking? A man in the middle of his prayers is a man in the presence of God. Such a man, were he to die at that moment, must fly to heaven, surely? Hamlet was about to send the murderer of his father to heaven! What kind of revenge was that?

Eyes staring in horror, the prince began to retreat, as noiselessly as he had advanced. This was not the moment to execute his uncle. He would wait until the man was in a drunken sleep, or a violent rage, or in the bed of sin he shared with Hamlet's mother. He would wait until he was gambling or swearing or flirting with one of the maids. Then the slain Claudius would go to the blackest deepest corner of hell, the place where he belonged.

Hamlet left the room. A moment later the king staggered to his feet, head throbbing. 'My words go to heaven but my thoughts stay here,' he whispered to himself. 'And words without thoughts bump upon the ceiling.'

TWENTY-ONE

Hamlet went down the stairs uneasily, still consumed by the memory ten minutes earlier of the king at prayer. He had found a lavatory and sat on it emptying his bowels in an exhausted rush. Perhaps he should have struck the king as he knelt, and left it to God to do the rest. But, when it came to carrying out the duties his father had set him, Hamlet knew there must be no mistake. His father had been a hard taskmaster. Critical whenever the boy had acted rashly or shown poor judgment, he would never forgive any error in this, the greatest challenge he had ever set his son, the greatest challenge any man could set his child.

As Hamlet walked along the corridor his feet slowed. He had the sense that he was walking towards feathers, and they would not be the comforting feathers contained within a mattress but rather they would be loose and uncontrolled. The air would be full of them and he would get them in his lungs every time he breathed. He had experienced this before, down in the poultry yard, and the memories slowed him further, until, about ten metres from his mother's door, he stopped and leaned against the wall, hugging himself with both hands under his armpits. His hands felt sticky with blood, and yet they were clean and pale.

He could hear his mother talking and a man's voice replying. The king! His uncle! Now the hotness of his thoughts just minutes earlier was cooling, and starting to confuse him. He began to regret this trip down the cold corridor. He could not bear to face both of them in her suite. He would not! His uncle had no business there, no right. He was the usurper. The son had more right than the husband. The prince's hand went to his sword again. Was this the right moment? Was it time? Could he do it in front of his mother?

The voices were quiet.

Trembling, Hamlet called out, 'Mother!' He wanted to warn the pair of them that he was coming. He wanted to avoid any scene that would disturb him further. He called again, 'Mother! Mother!' Even to himself he sounded querulous.

He opened the door and walked in. There she stood, one hand to her throat. Only four candles were lit in the great chandelier. The room was dim, the gold furniture glowed, the vases on the shelves were empty. She looked flushed. Hamlet was enraged by the sight of her but he kept his face icy.

'Why did you send for me?' he asked. He looked around the room. No sign of the king. He must have gone through the other door into the boudoir, the innermost chamber. Hamlet was blackened by rage. He was staggered by his own rage. That the uncle should be in there, while the mother talked to her son as though she had no thoughts of the usurper, as though she were pretending she did not know what was going on.

He looked back at her. He no longer trembled. He was sustained now by his sense of righteousness. He could see the great effort she made to speak to him calmly.

'Hamlet, you have much offended your father.'

Father? The lie had come so easily to her lips. That man had cuckolded his true father, the only one who had the right to the title.

'Mother, you have much offended my father.'

'Come, come,' she said, 'you answer with an idle tongue.'

'Go, go, you question with a wicked one.'

It was childish but he had never openly defied her before. The words almost stuck in his teeth. His mouth felt dry.

She was uneasy and embarrassed, and held her throat more tightly, as if to keep something in.

'What do you mean, Hamlet? You are not yourself. This is not the Hamlet I know.'

'You? Who are you? Do you know me?'

'Have you forgotten me?'

'No.' He spoke slowly, wanting her to remember every cut that he was about to inflict, every stinging slash across her face. 'No, I know who you are. You are Gertrude, the queen, your husband's brother's wife. And—I wish it were not so!—you are my mother.'

'That is enough. You have said enough.'

'I thought of you once as the soul of virtue,' he continued deliberately. 'I thought of you as the woman who modelled virtue. Now I know you for who you are. And I will tell you what you are.'

'Leave me, Hamlet. I don't like you when you're like this. Come back when you can be lovely again.'

'There are crimes that shriek to heaven to be avenged. Crimes that corrupt even the purest.'

'Go Hamlet, or I'll call the guards. You are ill. You are mad. You must go.'

Relentless, boring in on her, grey eyes arctic, he took her by the shoulders, and forced her back into a chair. 'You shall not budge,' he hissed at her. 'Now you shall hear it. You will not leave this room until I have held up a mirror that shows you what is within.'

She was frightened, and she tried to fight him off, to pull away the strong hands that held her. But his grip was too hard and she feared bruises that would disfigure her arms. 'What are you doing?' Her mask slipped and she cried out. 'Help me, someone, help. He's mad. He'll kill me. Stop it, stop it!'

From behind Hamlet came an echoing cry. 'Help! Help the queen!'

'By God,' he thought, 'there he is, hiding from me and spying on us. It is enough. If ever I was going to do it, I'll do it now.'

He let go of his mother, spun, with the speed that

had won him a hundred matches, and drew. Against the wall was the great half-finished tapestry of the death of Paris. The weaver from Russia had been working on it for eight months already. Behind it someone was struggling, caught up in the loom and the threads and the rolls. The fat king, surely. With a hoarse cry Hamlet ran his sword through Paris's shoulder, and on, into a soft body on the other side. On and on, forever, the sword ran, until it hit the wall. There was a sickly sweetness about the action which entranced Hamlet for a moment. A kind of ecstasy seized him, like the full-moon madness that led him to the pigpen. He stayed there, quivering, unable to move. A high-pitched scream came from the man and then a series of gasping sobs.

It is not the king, Hamlet thought. Does she have another lover? He pulled back, bringing his sword with him, and starting to shudder.

'What have you done?' his mother moaned. 'What have you done?'

Hamlet look at her stupidly. 'I don't know. Is it the king? Isn't it the king?'

She seemed incapable of answering. She closed her eyes and covered her face. He dropped his sword as though it were no use to him, and fought with the huge tapestry to move it. Eventually he had to pull it away from the wall. The sobs from behind it were now replaced by a soft noise, almost a whistling sound, as the last breaths left the body. Hamlet stepped around the tapestry and saw Polonius. The old man lay on his side, an unnaturally white hand flung out to his right, and a pool of sticky blood spreading across the floor. His eyes were closed.

He heard his mother sob, 'Oh God, Hamlet, what is to become of us?'

Staring at Polonius the young prince tried to imagine how he came to be there. He knew Polonius had not come to the apartment to make love: he was too feeble and sexless for that. It would be part of some scheme no doubt, another little conspiracy, another attempt to spy on Hamlet perhaps. This was the man who laid traps to ensnare everyone. It was his favourite hobby. Hamlet felt no pity for him. He could only think: this will teach him to stick his nose into other people's business. He went back out to where his mother was thrashing around on the chair, like a drowning woman.

'What have you done?' she hiccoughed. 'What mad and bloody deed is this!'

He was stung. His mind was still a mass of

conflicting thoughts. But to be attacked by her now, like this, it was too much. A rush and roar of blood filled his head. With a great sense of cutting a rope and watching himself drop down a mountainside, he replied, 'Yes, a bloody deed, bloody indeed, almost as bad, good mother, as killing a king, and marrying his brother.'

'Killing a king!' she gasped.

Hamlet was cold now, but white-faced and sweating. He picked up his sword and wiped it against the tapestry. The drops of blood on the ground, the smears on the material, these were familiar to him. They gave him strength for what he had to say. 'For you, mother, I have kept the sword of truth in my scabbard until now.'

'What have I done, that you say these things to me, Hamlet? How can I have earned your violence and your horrible words? I do not deserve this.'

'What have you done? Why, that's easy. Something that would cause a rose to turn into a wart, an act that spits in the face of the wedding vows, that embarrasses heaven itself. Mother, look at this.'

With one easy motion he lifted from the wall a small oil painting of two men. Gertrude had an uneasy feeling that perhaps he came in here often and took down the picture. Against a background of forest and mountain the men in the portrait stood, clad in thick warm robes, arms around each other in brotherhood. Hamlet pointed to the one on the left. 'Remember him, mother?' he enquired. His tone was of cold fury. 'Look at him. Look at him! Here are Mars and Jupiter, Hyperion and Mercury. Here is majesty indeed. It is in his face, his eyes, his bearing. Here is greatness. And beside him, what? This toad, this vermin, grumbling and grunting and shuffling through rooms that were made for finer stuff. How could you choose this over that? Where were your eyes, your ears, your senses? You must have sense, or you would not be taking breath now, but what kind of sense is it that chooses the rat over the stag? And don't tell me you fell in love. At your age, what can you know of the passion that lubricates love! It must have been judgment, but judgment of the devil indeed.'

He threw the painting onto the sideboard. The queen tried to answer him but as she was about to speak a trickle of blood ran across the floor between them. She groaned and covered her face again. Hamlet, not seeing it, was encouraged to go on. Waving his sword in the air, wanting to spear her but knowing he never could, he stabbed her again and again with words. Little impotent things but they would have to do. 'To take him into your bed, to give him access to that most sacred place, to besmear and besmirch yourself, to lie in his sweat while you exchange honeyed words…'

'Please Hamlet, enough, enough, please.'

'To make love with that bag of bloated flesh…'

'Hamlet, no more, I beg you!'

'Here you have a mountain, and here a pile of donkey shit…'

'Oh Hamlet, have you no pity, have you no understanding?'

'Without a thought of me, me, me…'

'Hamlet, I cannot bear it. I cannot look into my soul the way that you ask. I am afraid of what I may see. You show me such black and cancerous spots within, that my vision fails me. It is too much for anyone, too much for you even. For now, be concerned only with Polonius. It is enough, surely. Do something about Polonius.'

'Let the fat bag of guts lie there until I have your promise.'

'My promise?' she said, faintly. She could no longer deal with him.

'That you will not sleep with him,' the boy replied.

'That the next time he comes to your bed, you will send him away. Keep yourself pure, mother,' he begged. 'Please, you don't need him.'

She shook her head. He was too young. He did not understand anything. 'You have split my heart in two, Hamlet,' she began to say, but he cut her off again.

'Then throw away half of it, the rotten half. Keep only the half which is good.'

When she did not answer he took the silence to mean that she was beaten. He was satisfied that he had made his point. He had penetrated to her inner being and left his mark there. He felt exhausted, but triumphant. He had slain the serpent and barred its way to her bed, keeping her safe for his dead father and himself. After all, she was theirs. She belonged to them, not to the insidious nefarious pernicious cuckolding snake.

'You know I must go away?'

'Hamlet! I cannot speak of that with the old man lying there. All the blood. What do you take me for? I have feelings. I do not know you when you are in this state. Do something, please.'

Hamlet took her by the elbow and steered her into the next room. She was too frightened to resist

'This is not what I meant by doing something,' was all she could say.

'You know about my being sent away,' he demanded again, ignoring her emotions as much as he was ignoring the dead Polonius.

God, let him not be mad, she thought. Anything but madness.

'Sent away!' he demanded again.

'Yes, yes,' she said. 'You're going with Rosencrantz and Guildenstern. The king has commanded it. The old man had been telling me when you arrived.'

Hamlet was instantly suspicious. 'Rosencrantz and Guildenstern? What have they got to do with it?'

'Why, I think he said they are to keep you company…keep you safe.'

'They may have been my friends at school, but I trust them as much as I'd trust a pair of rats with a piece of pork. Knowing Claudius, he'll send me to some brigand to get me knocked off. I'll watch Rosencrantz and Guildenstern more closely than they could ever watch me. They may be in for a shock. A hangman's rope can fit the neck of the executioner as well as it fits the neck of the condemned man.'

The queen nodded, faint with fatigue. Hamlet did not appear to notice her condition. 'Polonius,' she said, her eyes closed.

This time he seemed to hear her. He went back to the first room. She followed and stood, one hand covering her mouth, as he took hold of the old man's body at the waist and swung it around so the head was against the wall. 'There'll be trouble with this one,' he remarked. 'He may weigh more in death than he did in life.'

Picking up the old bag of guts by the heels and dragging him behind, as a groom would take a sled of hay to the horses, he left the room.

TWENTY-TWO

To Horatio fell the melancholy task of telling Ophelia the news. Adolescence had changed their relationship, so that the easy familiarity of childhood had given way to a more awkward ebb and flow between them. Now every comment was charged with a different energy. But their affection for each other was still strong, and Horatio knew he was the right person to inform Ophelia that she was now orphaned.

He climbed the stairs to Polonius's apartment with his heart beating slowly but loudly. This was a well-worn staircase, the carpet completely split on many of the steps. As the king of conspiracy, the master of plots, the State Secretary of Gossip, Polonius had received many visitors.

Horatio passed through the reception rooms. They were cold and silent in the early morning. Everything here was severe, from the hard leather sofas to the bare tables, to the glass cabinets which stood in each corner, symmetrical and uncompromising. They contained Polonius's medals, certificates of commendation, letters of thanks from a dozen European monarchs. A black fur coat thrown roughly across a chair had the appearance of a dead animal. The fireplaces had not been cleaned from the night before.

Horatio trod softly, this messenger of death, ill-suited to his task, afraid to create any eddies, to disturb the air. At the end of the first room hung a large portrait of Polonius, glaring down at the boy who came in search of his daughter. In the second room, the heads of stags and wolves bared their teeth, as if defying Horatio to bring any more death into an apartment that was full of it. In the third room, gazing out of the window, was Ophelia.

Her white silk gown was so plain that Horatio, unknowing the ways of women, wondered if it was the garment she slept in. With no one to announce him, no warning of his coming, he already felt compromised. But then he remembered, to whom could she complain? Who was left to protect her? Who would come thundering into the room, waving his arms, remonstrating, admonishing Horatio for his intrusion? The closest person was Laertes, and he was in England.

Ophelia showed no signs of outrage. Indeed, she showed no signs of anything. She continued to gaze through the window. Horatio coughed gently, then, when she did not respond, cleared his throat more loudly. She turned to him and said, 'He has gone far away.'

'He…who has?' Horatio stammered. He decided that someone had already notified her of her father's death, and he felt relieved. Now he would not have to find the difficult words.

'Who has? What did I say? Pay no attention. Sometimes I dream.' Perfectly composed, she gazed at him. 'Are you here to see my father? I don't know where he is. He's normally at his desk by this hour. Writing his letters. Doing his business.'

He realised that he had been wrong: she had no idea of Polonius's death. Blood rushed to his face and he began to stammer again. 'Ophelia, I have…there has been…something terrible's happened.'

She sank down on a piano stool. She was so naturally pale that it was hard to imagine her becoming paler, but now her face was no longer even white; she lost all colour. 'Is it Hamlet?' she asked. As he hesitated with his answer, she turned to the piano, which was open, and, astonishingly, began playing a tune that he remembered from their childhood, though he did not know its name. It was a sweet and cheerful song that they used to sing on long walks, something about a blackbird in the snow.

When she finished the tune she closed the piano and walked to the window. Horatio was stupefied. He did not know what to say or how to act. She swung the window open, and then horrified him by climbing through it and sitting on the sill with her back to him. Cold air rushed into the room. Horatio started forward, then hesitated. Bound by the strict rules of etiquette that applied even between those who had been childhood friends, and despite his awareness that she no longer had a protector in the castle, he nonetheless was afraid to touch her.

'Ophelia!' he screeched, in a voice he had never heard from his mouth before. 'What are you doing? Nothing's happened to Hamlet.' Though even as he spoke he knew this was not true.

She glanced around at him. 'Do not fear,' she said. 'Say what you have come to say. Then I will stay, or fly away.'

He stared at her. 'Are you crazy? Come back inside. I'm not telling you anything while you're sitting like that. You're twenty metres from the ground.'

She immediately became very docile. She climbed back in at once and came towards him, head bowed, hands clasped in front of her. 'What do you have to tell me?' she muttered. 'Go ahead, say it. I'll be good.'

He took a deep breath, stood taller, and began. 'Ophelia, a terrible accident happened last night. Quite late. There was an awful scene in the queen's apartment. I'm still not sure of the details, but it seems that Hamlet…I think perhaps Hamlet mistook your father for an intruder…there was some kind of fight… well, I don't know how to tell you this, but…'

'He's dead, he's dead.' The girl began to rock herself. 'He killed him. I knew he would. Oh, I knew he would. Sweet Jesus. Sweet mother.'

'It's true, he is dead.'

'You said nothing had happened to him.'

Horatio realised she still had not understood the truth. He cursed himself for making such a mess of it. 'No, no, Ophelia, it's not Hamlet who has died, it's your father. Hamlet mistook him…there was some kind of terrible confusion…'

She fell back onto a sofa, her hands covering her face. 'Oh! My father! Then not Hamlet! Oh God forgive me, I did not want it to be Hamlet.' Suddenly she sat bolt upright, took her hands away, and stared at Horatio. 'Are you saying that Hamlet has killed my father?'

The boy nodded.

'He killed my father,' she whispered, unable to take her eyes from his face. 'Oh, better that he kill his own father. To kill a father! But God help me, I am as bad. The reek of this must reach to heaven itself. We will all be damned.'

'No, Ophelia, please, you cannot think like that. You must not. It was an accident. I don't know the details, but I'm sure that when it all comes out, we will find that Hamlet's honour remains intact.'

'Yes, yes, honour. That is everything. To keep honour intact. So, men fight. Oh, how little they know. How little they understand me. So, the young man must fight the old. They think that is the only way.'

Horatio did not know what she was talking about. He was greatly relieved when the door to his left opened and Ophelia's maid came in. Ophelia had never had a maid until recently, and Horatio did not even know the girl's name. She was from the north, daughter of a farmer, unused to the ways of the court, but Polonius had got her for nothing more than the cost of her board, in exchange for the promise of experience in serving a noble family. Well, Horatio thought, she'll get a lot more experience than she bargained for.

Seeing her mistress's distress, the maid hurried to her side. 'Madam,' she said, 'what is wrong?'

Ophelia turned away. Horatio, taking his opportunity, escaped, closing the door behind him and running through the other two reception rooms, desperate for space and open air.

That morning rumours flowed along the corridors of the castle like blood. Everyone whispered yet no one could be seen whispering, and so the pantries and anterooms and storerooms and cellars were full of servants and nobles, tradespeople and courtiers, children and pensioners, feeding each other with the food that cannot nourish. The king's sisters and cousins and aunts gathered in the banquet hall, too excited to eat, exchanging morsels and scraps of gossip instead. In the king's apartments Hamlet's uncle strode the carpet as the queen stood watching.

'Killed him?'

'Ran him through.'

'No excuse?'

'Not a jot.'

'It could have been me.'

'I fear so.'

'Why Gertrude, why?'

'He is mad.'

'And that's all?'

'Isn't that enough?'

'This is terrible.'

'It is, my lord.'

'They'll say it's us.'

The room was simply furnished, after the taste of Hamlet's father. Claudius and Gertrude had not yet indulged themselves as they had in her suite, with sumptuous carpets and lavish furnishings. Here, the floor of polished timber, two austere thrones made of a light white wood, and a dull red, padded sofa were lit by bright natural light through a row of large windows. Claudius always seemed ill-at-ease in the room, but never more so than now. He walked faster and faster, groaning and pulling at his beard, the sounds of his boots echoing like stones rattling on thick ice.

'They'll say we've been negligent. Or that we're part of a plot. They'll say we're responsible. We should have seen it coming. They'll say we should have sent him to a doctor, a hospital. That we used Hamlet to get rid of Polonius. They'll have us for bacon on their morning toast, Gertrude, unless we find a way to deal with this.'

'Yes.'

'Hamlet's too popular, that's the trouble. The people love him. He could get away with murder. Or so he thinks. To be loved by the mob, that's not a fate I'd wish on anyone. But it means we must be bloody careful.'

'They do love him,' the queen said pensively.

'Get the guard. I want Rosencrantz and Guilden-stern in here.'

When the two courtiers arrived the king barked at them. 'Are your bags packed?'

'Why no, Majesty, we had not realised…But it will take us no time to prepare…'

'Well, do it!' Then he had another idea. 'Wait! First,' he added, 'find the body and have it brought here. No, to the chapel.'

'Hamlet, Your Majesty?'

'No, no, you fool, not Hamlet, Polonius.' Claudius

threw himself down on his throne, and sat chewing a loose fingernail. 'Stop bowing!' he barked. 'Just go. Do what I told you!'

Rosencrantz and Guildenstern withdrew and began their melancholy search. Polonius was not in the queen's apartments, nor could they find a trail of blood or clue which might lead them to the old man's corpse. They did, however, find another body, of a sort. Hamlet was sitting on a bench looking out over the turrets at the distant forest. A bowl of coffee was at his feet. It looked untouched. The two men approached him cautiously. As usual, Rosencrantz did the talking.

'Excuse me, Your Royal Highness, might we have a word?'

'Certainly, certainly,' Hamlet said affably. 'What can I do for you?'

'Highness, we are charged by the king to find Polonius.'

'Ah, now there's a problem, right away.'

'There is?'

'Why, yes. You see the problem is that Polonius no longer exists. It therefore follows that your quest is doomed from the start. A shame, as I know how much you seek to gratify the king in all that you do.'

'Why yes, sir, he is in all things our ruler.'

'And you are a sponge.'

Rosencrantz had been moving forwards a little with each address to the prince but now he stopped. 'A sponge? Sir, do you mistake me for a sponge?' He glanced at Guildenstern as if to say, 'It's true, he's quite mad, next he'll tell us we're eggplants.'

But the prince was quite calm. 'Oh yes, sponges both of you, kept by the king to soak up his rewards, his orders, his moods, the spittle that drops from his lips. You soak them up, and when you are dripping with them, when you are saturated, then he squeezes you dry. You are his best servants, you sponges! And if not sponges you are the piece of apple in the corner of his mouth, which he chews and sucks on until he is ready to swallow it. But the problem is, how does a prince answer a sponge?'

Guildenstern: 'Highness, I do not understand you.'

Hamlet: 'I am glad of it.'

Rosencrantz: 'Sir, you must tell us where the body lies.'

Hamlet: 'Must! Is "must" a word to be used to princes, little man?'

Rosencrantz: 'Well, it is the king's wish that you tell us where the body lies.'

Hamlet: 'It does lie, that much is certain. No one ever got a true word out of him while he was alive and now he lies still.'

Rosencrantz: 'Your Royal Highness, Hamlet, please tell us where the body is and then go with us to the king.'

Hamlet: 'The body is already with the king, but not the king you are thinking of perhaps. And the king is not with the body. The king is a thing…'

Guildenstern: 'A thing? Sir, the king is a thing?

Hamlet: A thing of nothing. Bring me to him.'

TWENTY-THREE

Claudius was distraught, unable to fix on a plan, an easy answer. He liked life to be obvious. 'Hamlet's too popular with the people,' he told his wife again. 'Just because he's good-looking, that's all it is. But it makes him dangerous. He could kill their grandmothers, and as long as he keeps smiling at them and kissing their babies they'll forgive him. The people didn't love Polonius, but as long as he was around they felt secure. We have to get rid of Hamlet, but we must do it so it looks all right.'

'Get rid of him!' exclaimed the queen, showing for the first time an interest in the king's fretful monologue. 'Get rid of him?'

'No, no, I don't mean like that. I told you, I've arranged for Rosencrantz and Guildenstern to go away with him. But it mustn't look like a cover-up. We'll send him early, but we'll say it's for his own protection. And we'll set up an enquiry, so it looks as though we're doing something. In the meantime, while we're establishing the terms of reference and so forth, he shall be sent to a safe place. Further than England. To Australia. No, he'll end up marrying some unsuitable girl. To Nepal. No, not Nepal. Bad idea. To the moon.'

'I fancy England will be far enough.'

'Yes, all right, England then. Yes, as long as it looks as though we're just bringing his trip forward. He must go now, straight away. England will do nicely, I think. Keep him out of mischief and away from us.'

At that moment Hamlet entered the room and the king wondered if the young man had heard his last comment. The prince looked composed, but a flush in his cheeks and a brightness in his eyes gave the appearance of someone who had just come in from playing a game of football, or skiing down a fast and dangerous slope. Claudius hurried forwards. Behind Hamlet came Rosencrantz and Guildenstern,

Rosencrantz signalling that they were returning empty-handed: they had not found the body.

Claudius was genial. 'Now, Hamlet, we can't have this. Where's Polonius?'

Deadpan, Hamlet replied, 'At supper.'

'At supper?'

'Yes, there's a regular feast going on and Polonius is at the centre of it.'

The king was still baffled until Hamlet pressed on. 'The worms are having a great supper, and Polonius is their special treat this night.'

The king shook his great head and groaned. 'Have you completely taken leave of your reason?' But all attention was on the prince, and it was not clear whether anyone heard the cry from Claudius's heart.

Hamlet continued without pause. 'This is the thing about worms—we fatten all other creatures so that we might fatten ourselves, but worms, and worms alone, grow fat on us. The worm is the most democratic of creatures. The fat king and the lean beggar are one and the same to him.'

'I will not hear this,' Claudius said to Gertrude in a roaring whisper.

'Hush, let him finish. We need to find the old man.'

'A beggar who goes fishing may use a worm which has feasted on a king as his bait,' said Hamlet blithely. He was now moving around the room like a philosopher developing an argument, at times gazing out through the heavy stained-glass windows as if seeking an answer in the filtered light. 'And the fisherman may eat the fish caught with that bait. What does this tell us? Well, it tells us that a king may progress through the guts of a pauper.'

The queen laid an urgent hand upon her husband's arm; nothing else would have stopped him from running across the room and throwing himself on his stepson.

'Thus,' said Hamlet, 'we understand the democratic nature of the worm. In him all people are united; in him all people are made equal; the wise become foolish and the foolish wise.'

'WHERE IS POLONIUS?' roared the king.

'Polonius? You wish to be better acquainted with Polonius? Well then, you had better send a messenger to heaven, and if your messenger does not find him there, go and look for him in hell yourself.'

'By heavens I'll send you to hell, and soon enough,' growled Claudius, then glanced around guiltily. Gertrude clutched his arm more tightly.

Hamlet smiled at his mother. 'If a month or so passes, however, and you still have not found the old man, I suggest you try the mezzanine that is reached by the southern staircase. You may smell him as you pass the red door.'

Claudius sagged back in his throne. It seemed almost too light to support him. He waved to Rosencrantz and Guildenstern. 'Go and look in the mezzanine.'

As the two young men departed, Hamlet remarked equably to them, 'He will stay there till you come.'

Through hooded eyes the king gazed at him. 'Hamlet, you have put yourself in a dangerous position by this—shall we say—unfortunate accident. You know how much your mother and I care for your safety. We put it above our own even. We need to get you out of the country. Prepare for a long journey! I will arrange a boat, I will arrange letters, I will arrange a couple of associates for you, I would arrange a favourable wind if I could! You must be ready to leave today—for England.'

'For England?' Hamlet echoed, as though he had never heard of the place.

'Yes.'

'Fine. Good.'

'So it is good, for my purposes,' said Claudius.

'I know an angel who knows your purposes. And the angel is not Rosencrantz and he is not Guildenstern. But come, for England. I will be off.' He went to the king and performed the elaborate bow that etiquette required. 'Farewell, dear mother,' he said to him.

'I am your loving father, Hamlet,' Claudius said, startled and embarrassed.

'My mother,' replied the prince. 'Father and mother is man and wife, man and wife are a unity, so you are my mother.'

He bowed again and, without even looking at his mother, much less saying goodbye to her, he swiftly left the room. The king watched him go. His eyes were mere slits now and he muttered into his beard. Only he heard the words, but they did not bode well for his young nephew.

TWENTY-FOUR

And so Hamlet, aware that he had created a situation too unstable for his own good, appreciating the need for some clear air, sailed for England, with his two loving friends, Rosencrantz and Guildenstern.

And then Ophelia went mad.

No one could name the day or even the hour when it happened, but it soon became apparent that her beautiful mind was gone.

One afternoon the queen found herself caught in a distressing conversation with Osric, the young farmer who had attached himself to Claudius. He entered the room with much dramatic staring, apparently checking for spies and eavesdroppers. Satisfied that his great announcement could be made in confidence he began the kind of fawning approaching-members-of-the-royal-family dance that he imagined was not just appropriate but elegant as well. Gertrude gazed at him through impatient eyes, wondering how long this praying mantis manoeuvre might take. 'Really,' she thought, 'the only people who truly know how to behave at court are the ones who have been here all their lives. It can't be taught. Especially to people like this fool.'

She longed for an honest conversation. But Osric was too excited to complete his performance. He began speaking before he had finished his second bow. 'Your Majesty, Ophelia craves an audience with you, and is so distracted that I thought it best to come here at once.'

'An audience with me? Does she need help? She can visit me any time she wants, within reason. Although, come to think of it, it's been some days since I saw her around the castle.'

'Ah, Majesty, that is the thing, until today she has been seeing no one and for that matter eating nothing. But she has a sudden fixed idea that she must see you.' Now Osric had done with his bowing and he came close, uncomfortably close, to the queen. He launched into his news. 'Majesty, it is my belief that she has lost her reason.'

'Lost her reason?' Fear stole into Gertrude's heart, an icy trickle of fear. 'I hope you are wrong!'

'Your Majesty, she has emerged from her apartments and after talking to no one is now talking to everyone. She speaks all the time of her father, is angry and confused and full of strange hints and troubled comments. At one moment she says there are tricks and plots in the world, the next she is winking and nodding and poking at people as though they all share in some guilty secret. Then people try to guess what she is about, and at times, ma'am, you would hardly credit their guesses. It makes them think the wildest thoughts.'

The queen had wild thoughts herself at this news. 'You had better bring her in,' she said slowly.

The last thing the king and she needed was a castle full of rumours and out-of-control whispers. Gertrude's life was now so full of dark places that she shied at everything. Her conscience had made her over-sensitive. She should have spent more time with Ophelia after the death of Polonius. She had seen Ophelia's distress shortly after the stabbing. The girl was wild-eyed, on the edge of hysteria. At the funeral Gertrude had stood with her, held her, whispered to her, encouraged her to stay strong. But only now did she realise that she had never been alone with her since the dreadful night of the stabbing. Gertrude had no daughter, just a son, but the motherless Ophelia was the closest she had to a daughter. There was every reason to suppose that one day Ophelia would become her daughter-in-law. But Gertrude's behaviour had not been that of a good mother. There had been no time in the emotional storms that blew constantly around Elsinore these days. It was Hamlet, everything was Hamlet, he had turned every life in the castle upside down with his disregard for everyone but himself.

Gertrude gazed nervously out of the window, trying to decipher the night outside. When she turned at a sound from the doorway it seemed to her that the room had become much darker. Ophelia, wandering towards her, was like a white swan glimpsed in twilight, with feathers disordered and head averted.

The queen felt instant pity. Ophelia looked so distressed and unwell.

'Where is the beauteous majesty of Denmark?' Ophelia asked, wringing her hands and lifting a woebegone face to Gertrude. She began to sing.

He is dead and gone, lady,
He is dead and gone.
At his head a grass–green turf
At his heels a stone.

As Ophelia sang, the queen, however, hardened her heart. The girl just needed a good talking-to. She had to pull herself together, before she made trouble for all of them. Everyone had problems, that was the way of it, and it was no good to let them weigh you down until they drowned you. That didn't help anyone. If Hamlet were to be king one day, and Ophelia by his side as queen, she would need to be made of stern stuff. 'Ophelia, what silly words are these?' the queen began, thinking at the same time: is she really speaking of her father? Since when did Polonius become the beauteous majesty of Denmark?

But Ophelia held up a hand so imperious that Gertrude could not go on. As though taking the queen into her confidence, she whispered:

Who has sent him to the grave?
Who has dug him deep?
Why, the ones who know him best
And ought his soul to keep.

We can't have this, thought the queen. For once Osric is right in his report.

'My dear child,' she began, but was interrupted again, this time by Claudius entering the room. He had been in a better frame of mind since driving off Hamlet. If England dealt with the prince as he had asked he might never have to see that pretty head again. He might be out of the woods. So he came in whistling, his red round face shining with eagerness to tell his wife of the nine-point stag he had brought down that very morning.

'Ah, who have we here? Ophelia! Where have you been hiding yourself? Mourning for your dear father? Well, most proper, but you are equally proper to emerge from your seclusion now, especially among us, your dear friends. Fathers die you know, that is the way of it. Grief can be ungodly, remember.'

Only now, after he had sat down and arranged his robes, did he see Gertrude's warning frown and warning finger. He halted, puzzled. What did they have to fear from Ophelia?

The young woman appeared not to notice the king at first. She sang on:

White his shroud, as the morning snow,
White as his heart so pure,
Red the blood that they cruelly spilt,
For them there will be no cure.

'What is all this, Ophelia?' The king was trying to maintain his jovial mood, though he felt it ebbing fast. He did not understand what was going on here, and he did not like what he did not understand.

'Well, God reward you,' Ophelia said, but without looking at him or seeming to see anyone in the room. 'I'll tell you a story I heard once, a story of St Valentine's Day, about a faithful young woman, knowing the tradition that whoever a man sees first when the day dawns will be his true love ever after, placed herself by his window the night before and waited till dawn. What do you think happened? Why, he never looked out the window, but opened his door and let in the maid. And she was no maid by the time she left his room again. Ah, perhaps I should have let him raise his tent.'

'What on earth is she talking about?' the king muttered angrily to his wife.

'I have no idea. Don't look at me as though it's my fault, that stupid Osric brought her in, said she was talking wildly and starting rumours. I thought I had better check up on what crazy stories she might be spreading.'

'This is all we need. How long has she been like this?'

'How should I know? Ask Osric. Apparently he's become the expert on life at Elsinore. Ask her ladies-in-waiting.'

Ophelia had wandered away to the window and now was talking to no one. Not anyone who could be seen, at any rate. 'Oh, pity the fate of a maiden! If she lets him take her, she is deserted. If she doesn't, she is deserted. I hope all will be well. We must be patient but I cannot choose but weep, to think they should lay him in the cold ground. My good brother shall know of it, and so I thank you for your wise advice. Come, my coach! Good night, ladies, good night, good night. Good night, sweet ladies.'

She drifted out of the room by the western door. Claudius nodded to a couple of his wife's attendants.

'Follow her closely, keep a sharp eye on her.'

TWENTY-FIVE

With a wave and a nod of dismissal, Claudius cleared the room of the other courtiers. He and Gertrude were left alone. The king turned to his wife. His good mood had been confettied and blown to Norway. 'This is the poison of deep grief. It springs from her father's death. Honestly, Gertrude, when troubles come they come, not as single soldiers but as battalions, as armies. First her father slain, then your son gone—the author of his own downfall, but of course the people don't know that. It's started trouble and rumours and unrest from one end of the kingdom to the other.'

Claudius tapped his finger against his teeth. 'We did the wrong thing with Polonius, burying him so quickly. We should have given him a state funeral, put his old carcass on a slab for a couple of days, invited the masses to come and see him. Only the stickybeaks would have bothered, but the people would have got the message, that we have nothing to hide. Instead, we've got a mood like mud, thick and unwholesome mud. And now, as if that's not enough, you give me Ophelia! I thought you were meant to be looking after her! I come in here, after a good day out on the hills, and what do I find? A girl divided from herself, lost her judgment…and without judgment, Gertrude, we are no better than the beasts. We are mere pictures. We are two-dimensional.

'And to top it all off, Laertes is sneaking back into the country from England and won't listen to any accurate accounts of how his father died. He's already crossed the border, and is ignoring all my messages. Needless to say, without any facts to go on, he won't hesitate to blame everything on us, on me. Gertrude, this castle, this kingdom, is more like a crime scene than a sovereign state.'

A thumping and yelling from the courtyard inter-rupted him. The noise rolled through the room like echoing thunder. Boots running, more boots stomping up the stairs, more shouts. An angry voice: 'You try to stop them then!' Someone else shouted: 'Well, he lives here!'

'What's going on?' Gertrude gripped the arms of her chair and sat up.

'Good God, it sounds like a riot.' Both king and queen sprang to their feet. 'Guards! Guards!' The king strode towards the door. 'GUARDS!'

A captain hurried into the room, hat askew, eyes staring. 'Your Majesty, Laertes is here at the head of a crowd of supporters. They've stormed past the outer defences, it seems. There's a whole crowd of them calling for Laertes to be made king.'

'King? Laertes?'

'Majesty, I fear so. It's as though tradition and law are suddenly of no account. As though the world is just opening its eyes to its first day, and suddenly history has no meaning. "Laertes shall be king!" They sound like a pack of dogs howling to the clouds.'

'A false pack of dogs indeed,' snarled Gertrude. She put her hand to her throat as the king advanced on the captain. 'They're following the wrong trail.'

'Of course, Your Majesty.'

Another guard rushed in. 'They've broken down

the doors!' he cried. Three more guards followed, then, suddenly, a whole vomit of them. In among their red and grey uniforms came other colours, the purples and greens of the courtiers, pinks and whites and violets of ladies-in-waiting, scarlets and blues of palace servants, black-suited clerks.

Claudius, always formidable in a fight, retreated to his throne and stood in front of it, hands on hips. The queen sank back onto her chair, aware that she could pull no strings here, play no role, have no influence. All she could do was watch and wait for the scene to play itself out.

Noise hubbled and bubbled into the room. As the crowd got bigger and pushed in further, the noble colours of those who resided at court gave way to grubbier clothes, greys and browns and blacks. The first wave, members of the royal household, forgetting protocol, no longer in control of their lives, had their backs to the royal couple, watching anxiously to see what their future might look like. The second wave all looked forwards, with sharp and hungry eyes.

In the middle of them, like a young conqueror, through the huge oak doors, bright and excited, strode Laertes.

'Where is the king?' he shouted, and then,

self-consciously, added, 'Oh there you are.' He turned to the crowd. 'Give me space, I beg you. I need to talk to the king.'

'No, no!' they shouted at him.

'Yes, please, I entreat you, I am here to speak of my father. If you honoured him, then let me have this time to speak to the only man who can answer my questions.'

Scowling, reluctant, but having to acknowledge his rights, the crowd began to withdraw. The guards, sensing the change in mood, began to move against them, applying pressure around the edges. The Elsinore residents and staff, too, started to shuffle away. In a short time only three people were left in the room.

Laertes, trembling with excitement, faced the older man. Both were red-faced, chests puffed forwards, staring at each other. 'Oh, vile king,' he exclaimed, 'give me my father.'

'Be calm, Laertes,' Claudius urged.

'Calm! Calm! If there is a single drop of blood in me that is calm, then that drop of blood says that I am not my father's son. That drop of blood says my mother is a slut, who slept with someone else to get me. I will not be calm.'

In a frenzy of rage he grabbed the king by the

front of his robe. The queen leapt to her feet and opened her mouth to call for the guards. But Claudius, who liked the physical as much as he hated battles of words and wit, disentangled himself and gestured to her to sit again. 'Have no fear, Gertrude,' he said. 'A king is surrounded by the protection of God himself. When faced by true royalty, treason can only blink. Now, Laertes, tell me, what troubles you? What is the cause of such massive rage?'

'Where is my father?'

'Dead.'

'But not killed by the king,' Gertrude interrupted. Again Claudius waved her away.

'How did he die?' Laertes demanded. 'I won't be juggled with. If God protects you, then I say to hell with God, to hell with my vows of loyalty, I say that my allegiance to the throne of Denmark can go to the blackest devil. My father was loyal to me and I return that loyalty now. I don't care if I stand in the deepest pit of the fieriest furnace—as long as I get revenge.'

'Tell me this,' said the king, his voice rumbling from deep in his chest, 'is your desire for revenge so overwhelming that you don't care who you attack? Will both friend and foe fall to your avenging sword?'

'Of course not. His enemies only.'

'Will you know his enemies then? And his friends?'

'I'll embrace his friends warmly. They will be my honoured guests.'

'Ah! Now you speak like a good son and a true gentleman.'

Laertes opened his mouth to respond but another disturbance in the doorway distracted him. He looked around and was astonished to see his sister enter. She drifted in like a wisp of mist in the late afternoon. Laertes' mouth stayed open. It was obvious that Ophelia was deranged. She wafted around the room with no sign that she was aware of her brother's presence. For two or three minutes Laertes watched, unable to speak. In that time he seemed to age ten years.

Ophelia began singing:

> They took him to the graveyard near,
> And laid him in his bed,
> Upon his corpse as he lay there
> How many a tear was shed.

Finally Laertes made his mouth work again. 'Oh, sweet Ophelia! Oh, dear kind sister! It is possible that the mind of a young woman could be as fragile as an old man's life? Could nature have sent a part of her to accompany our father? Oh heat, dry up my brains! Oh, let my tears be thick with salt and burn out my eyes so that I do not have to look upon this sad sight.'

'There's rosemary,' Ophelia said suddenly. 'That's for remembrance. Remember that, love. There are pansies—they're for thoughts. There's fennel and columbines for the queen. Some say they speak of unfaithfulness, but what would I know of that? There's rue for you, sir, the king sir, to show you repent, if indeed you do. There's rue for me, for my sadness. We may call it the herb of grace on Sundays. I would give you a daisy, for love, and some violets, for faithfulness, but they withered when my father died. They say he made a good end…

> And will he not come again?
> And will he not come again?
> No, no he is dead.
> Go to your deathbed.
> He never will come again.
>
> His beard was as white as snow,
> All flaxen was his head,

He is gone, he is gone,
He is on his cold bed,
And to my cold bed I will go.

Still singing her mournful song Ophelia eddied out of the room. The melody could be heard for a long time as she drifted down the staircase.

'Oh, dear sister,' Laertes muttered, 'if your mind was whole and you had a thousand words to persuade me to seek revenge you would not be more successful than you are now.'

TWENTY-SIX

Laertes, head in hands, was slumped on the edge of the platform on which the two thrones sat. He looked up and met the king's eyes.

'Does God see this?' he groaned. 'How can he allow such offence to all that is fair?'

'Laertes,' said Claudius urgently. 'We are in this together. We are on the same side. If you ever find that the queen and I conspired in any way to do you harm, you can have my kingdom. You don't have to ask for it. I will give you everything: crown, castles, treasure. My life even. Have it, take it. Instead of blaming us, find your true enemy. And, where the offence is, there let the great axe fall.'

'I know you're speaking of Hamlet. But if it is true that he took my father's life, why have you let him go free?'

'Laertes, good Laertes.' The king helped him stand, then walked him down the room, away from the queen's hearing. They stopped in front of a giant portrait that hung on the southern wall. It showed a Madonna cradling the body of her crucified son. 'Magnificent, isn't it?' said the king. 'It was a gift from the old King Fortinbras of Norway, twenty years ago. Grandfather to the Fortinbras who pecks at our borders now.'

The king turned and faced the young man.

'Laertes, you should know, one of my problems in dealing with Hamlet is his mother. She worships the ground he walks on. To her, he can do no wrong. And the queen is so conjunctive to my life and soul that I revolve around her—like a star moving in an orbit which cannot be altered. It is my virtue and my plague that I am so dependent upon her. But the same problem exists with the general population. Hamlet is loved by the common people. He is the pet of the public! If I put him on trial…well, my arrows, aimed against him, would turn back on me and deliver me a mortal wound. Don't you understand that? My position is not what you think.'

'And so I lose my father. And now my sister too, it seems, is slipping away.'

'No, no, you underestimate me. I have made arrangements which I think you will smile upon. You may not have heard that I despatched Hamlet to England. In the company of those fine fellows Rosencrantz and Guildenstern. Now there's a pair of conspirators if you like! Who knows what they might get up to in England, with their royal charge.'

'Your Majesty is mistaken,' said Laertes coldly, sniffing for a plot closer to home. 'Hamlet is not a hundred miles from Elsinore.'

'I think not,' said the king, smiling. 'He will have arrived at his final destination by now. His final destination—do you understand what I mean? I am waiting for news from England that Hamlet is—let me put it delicately, in his mother's presence—that Hamlet is most finally arrived.'

'Whilst you are waiting for that news you might speak to Horatio, my lord. Horatio has in his hand a letter from Hamlet advising that he has just landed in Denmark after a devilish bad voyage. I believe he abandoned Rosencrantz and Guildenstern in Calais, giving them strict instructions to continue their journey to England without him.'

Claudius staggered where he stood and gaped at the young man. 'Can this be true?'

'Horatio recognises the writing and the letter is blood-red with the prince's seal.'

The king threw back his head and roared like a lion. Spittle flew from his mouth. Laertes stepped back. Claudius tore away from him and paced up and down the floor, swinging his cloaks about him. The queen, wisely, slipped out of the room. After two agitated minutes Claudius turned again to Laertes and bellowed at him. 'Then you shall have your revenge! On the one who is the instrument of all your misfortunes! I'm not so feeble that I'll allow people to pull my beard while I sit there giggling at their play. Have your revenge. And I will have mine!'

'Then hurry, Hamlet, to Elsinore,' Laertes growled back. 'It warms the sickest parts of my soul that I will soon be able to say to him, "Now your turn has come!"'

'Wait! Wait!' The king strode to the door and checked that they were unobserved. 'Softly, my dear fellow. If you will be ruled by me on this…'

Laertes bowed his head. 'Majesty, you are my king.'

'Good. Then do as I say. We will fix this so that, whatever happens to Hamlet, no blame can fall on either of us, you especially.'

'Is that possible?'

'Certainly. I have an idea already. I remember reports that you are much improved in swordsmanship since you went to France?'

Laertes nodded.

'Good. That's a start. Now, Laertes, let me ask you this. Did you love your father? Or, are you merely a painting of sorrow? A face without a heart?'

'How can you ask?'

'Oh, I know you loved him. But love is controlled by time, dear Laertes. There lives in the flame of love a kind of gas that will abate it. Just as a candle has its wick, no matter how bright the flame burns, sooner or later the wick gives out and the flame dies. What we would do, we should do. But "would" soon gets eaten away by the cancers of time and change and words and indecision. How far are you prepared to go to show that you are truly your father's son?'

'I would cut Hamlet's throat in church,' said Laertes, without blinking, without a tremor. 'In front of the altar, with Christ looking on. Does that satisfy you?'

'Well, you're right,' said the king. But even he blinked and trembled at the savagery of the younger man's rage. 'You're right, of course. There should be no place sacred against a murderer. Not when you are acting properly, for the honour of your family. Even a church. Well, well. But as I was saying, let us try to be more subtle. When Hamlet does reach here, why don't you keep to your own apartments and let us devise a plan. We'll cast out a bait and let him rise to it. When the time is right, we'll organise a sword fight. He's such a trusting fellow, we can accidentally leave the protector off the tip of the sword, so instead of a hit leaving nothing but a faint mark, you'll run him through. How's that for a plan?'

'I'll do better than that,' Laertes snarled. 'I have a poison I bought from an old witch in a back room in Marseilles. It's lethal enough to shrivel a tree and send the leaves falling. I'll daub the tip of the sword with it. One scratch with that and he can call to the highest heaven for help, but nothing on earth or beyond it will save him.'

'Good, good. Anything we can do to make this a certainty is worth doing. We can't afford to fail, dear Laertes. In fact I have some poison too, a concoction I have used only once, to get rid of an old bull. A sniff of it would despatch a wayward calf.' Claudius burst into a fit of coughing, and had to wipe his eyes and blow his nose before he could go on. 'I'll add it to Hamlet's wine glass. A bit of hot sword-fighting, a pause while he takes a drink, and if you can't scratch him with your weapon then, as his limbs become sluggish with the venom, you are not the duellist whose praises I have heard sung throughout Denmark!'

'I'll do it,' said Laertes, fervent and red-eyed. He clasped the king's hand in a double grip, and the two men clenched fists until their fingers were white and bloodless. Then, satisfied with their afternoon's work, they went their separate ways, each smouldering, each ready to burst into flames.

TWENTY SEVEN

The cemetery had not changed much. It would be a
wonder if it had. Hamlet approached it slowly, keeping
to one side of the path, barely visible to travellers on
the road. There were none anyway. He had not
intended to pay the graveyard a visit but something
within him dragged at his legs and sought distraction,
wanted to delay his arrival at the castle. That impulse
turned him sideways so that he found himself standing
at the foreigners' gate. There was activity in the distance, beside the old quince tree that marked the
southern boundary, but the morning mist had not
cleared; indeed, now, in mid-afternoon, it was heavier

than ever. Hamlet could see the figure of a man, working at one of the grave sites, but he could not recognise him at this distance. 'Probably that old bearded fellow,' the prince thought. 'Or has someone buried him now, and replaced him at his melancholy task?'

He opened the gate and wandered in, manoeuvring among the gravestones until he was closer to the labourer. It was indeed the same gravedigger Hamlet had seen at his father's funeral. His beard was at least a foot longer than Hamlet remembered, and he was shovelling the loamy soil. He was in it up to his shoulders, almost, and as he was a lanky brute it meant that the grave was nearing completion. He flung out another load. The lift needed was tremendous, and Hamlet was impressed that he could still manage it at his age. Most gravediggers would have used a pulley.

'Who's there?' the man said, squinting through rheumy eyes.

His arms may be strong, Hamlet thought, but his eyes are failing. 'Just a traveller,' the prince replied. His words were turning to mist. 'Whose grave is that?'

'Why it's mine, sir. Whose do you think it would be? There are nigh on ten thousand who reside in this place and two thousand and twenty rest in graves of my making.'

'That's a fine tally.'

'It is indeed, sir, and I'm hoping to add to them. It's a funny thing, but people keep dying, and so my score increases.'

'Do you think they'll ever stop?'

'I don't, sir, and that's a fact.' The man was leaning on his shovel now and wheezing. It seemed that the break in his labours had come at the right time. 'No, sir, not until the day of judgment, when they'll disturb the earth and put all my work to naught. What a mess the place will be on that day, sir. I often think of that.'

'I suppose so.' Hamlet smiled to himself. 'But tell me, who will be buried in this grave?'

'Why, someone dead, sir, to be sure. It'd be a terrible thing if it were anyone else.'

Hamlet smiled again. He walked over to peer into the pit. 'It's a fearful deep hole.'

'It is, sir, yet some of them are in a rush to get into it. The young lady who will be lodged in it presently, now she were in a terrible rush, sir. And it were in the rushes they found her, where she'd drowned herself.'

'Not her fault though, I suppose,' Hamlet said. 'It must have been an accident, or they would hardly be burying her in this holy ground.' A tremble ran through him, knowing how close he himself had come to self-slaughter. 'To those who deliberately end the lives God has given them, a special place is reserved.'

'Aye, sir, that it is, and the earth is extra cold where they are buried, sir, out by the forest, so they may feel even more warmly the flames for which they're bound. I could take you there, sir, if you like. There's some who like to see it.'

Hamlet shivered at the morbid thought. He went to turn away but his foot brushed something. He looked, and saw a skull leering up at him. Curious, he bent and picked it up. 'What's this?' he asked the old gravedigger.

'Well now I can't quite see what you have there, traveller. My sight is as short as my years are long.'

'It's a skull.'

'No surprise in that, sir,' the man said, reaching out for it. 'Where are you more likely to find a skull than in a graveyard? Still, he's a bit too eager for the day of judgment, that one. Give it here, sir, and I'll pop him back where he belongs.'

'How long do they last before they rot?' asked the prince, still holding onto the grisly object.

'Well now, sir, a lot of them are rotten before they

come here. Some of them are so riddled with the pox that it's a job to hold them together long enough to get them into the ground. But if they're not poxy then they last about eight or nine years. Nine years for the tanners.'

'Why do the tanners last longer?'

'A tanner, his hide is already so tanned with his trade, that he keeps out the water. And it's the water that rots them. A human can have too much water. Like the young lady that's bound for this hole.'

Hamlet grimaced. Suddenly he was conscious of the weight of his head, compared to that of the skull he was holding. 'This fellow, who is he, do you know?'

'He's nobody now, sir. No body, do you get it?'

'All right, well who was he?'

'I can guess who he was, without even looking at him. If he came out of this grave, and it's fair to suppose he did, he'd have to be Yorrick, jester to the king. Things are a little crowded around here, sir, as you may have noticed. Dying's a fearful popular activity these days, so we often double 'em up, and then some. There's plenty of graves here with half a dozen in them. I thought we might run into Yorrick sooner or later. No doubt there's a good bit more of him around my feet.'

'Yorrick?' the prince repeated, gripped by horror. 'Yorrick you say?' He gazed at the skull trying to see something familiar in it, trying to find the sharp nose, the ruddy cheeks, the quick laugh. The empty eye sockets stared back at him, seeing nothing. Hamlet shook his own head. 'Where are your jokes now, merry man?' he whispered to the skull. 'Where are your riddles and your limericks? Where are your musical farts? Is this the fate of all men? Alexander the Great, too, Julius Caesar, Shakespeare, do you all come to this?'

There was no reply.

The gravedigger shrugged. 'Talk to him as much as you want, sir. But let me have him back when you've grown tired of the conversation. There's a funeral to be had, and I think I hear them coming already. They're a little early and I'm a little late, but if we've reached Yorrick I'd say we're deep enough.'

He sprang out of the grave with amazing agility. Embarrassed, Hamlet handed him the skull and the man threw it back into the pit. He had been right about the funeral procession. Now Hamlet too could hear the soft tolling of the horse bells, although the mist still obscured the people from view. He marvelled at the keen hearing of the old fellow.

Visited by irresistible curiosity, Hamlet grabbed the gravedigger by the sleeve. 'You say she drowned?'

'Drowned herself, yes, sir. In tears and the river.'

'But by accident, surely?' Hamlet insisted. Something in the man's manner niggled at him.

'Well now, sir, some would say that.'

'You mean it is possible that she ended her own life? Deliberately?'

'Now now, sir, enough, they are almost upon us and I have work to do.'

TWENTY-EIGHT

Hamlet, his curiosity not satisfied, resolved to linger. He retired to a row of young elms behind the last graves and peered into the mist. The procession had reached the main entrance to the cemetery. Hamlet could see the men unloading the coffin from the hearse. This was a high-born person then; ordinary citizens like Yorrick got no such luxuries as a box to protect their tender flesh.

The priest was opening the gate. He propped it open then led the way towards the new pit. Behind the robed figure Hamlet was transfixed to see the king himself, his treacherous uncle, followed by the queen, then a group of servants from the palace carrying the pale coffin.

Looming out of the mist behind them was Laertes, accompanied by another priest. As the coffin and the royal couple took the path that would bring them to the front of the grave, Laertes and the second priest diverged onto the other path, which would take them to the grave's head. But they stopped, just metres away from Hamlet, and began a conversation in angry whispers. Every word went straight to the prince's ears, burning as though they were frost.

Laertes: 'What other ceremonies are to be observed?'

Priest: 'We cannot do any more. We have already gone as far as we dare.'

Laertes: 'But what other ceremonies?'

Priest: 'Had it not been for the queen's orders we would not have done as much as this. Were it not for her majesty she should have lain in unblessed ground until the day of judgment. Instead of prayers she would have had rocks thrown at her grave. Here she has flowers. Be grateful for that much at least.'

Laertes: 'So you'll do nothing else for her?'

Priest: 'We would be in savage breach of the church's rules to say prayers over the grave. Such a privilege is for those who have departed their lives in peace.'

Laertes: 'Let me tell you this, you sour and miserable minister of God: plant her fair and uncorrupted body in the earth and watch the violets grow from her. My sister shall be an angel ministering to others while you lie howling in hell.'

Slow fear had been growing inside Hamlet while the two men were talking. Now the fear flowered into a garden of huge and terrifying cactus plants. Each plant shouted the name 'Ophelia' at him. The prince tore at his throat as if to rip out every word he had ever said to his beloved.

The queen was already scattering flowers over the coffin, which had been lowered into its home in indecent haste. 'Sweets to the sweet,' she crooned. 'I thought I would have been weaving flowers for your wedding to my son, not throwing them in your grave.'

Laertes and the priest had advanced towards them. Laertes, his temper already stirred by the priest's churlish words, came to the boil at the mention of Hamlet. Springing forwards, in a voice barely recognisable, he cried: 'A hundred curses on that miserable name, the one who sent my sister mad. Ophelia, I cannot let them cover you in earth.'

Before anyone realised his intention he leapt straight into the grave. A cracking noise gave those gathered around the pit the terrible thought that he might have burst the coffin but it was not that, just the impact of his feet and some falling rocks on the wood. 'Bury me with her,' he sobbed. 'Please! Pile the earth on both of us.'

Hamlet began to advance from the shadows. He was deaf and blind to the feelings of Laertes. He could think of nothing but his own despair. 'Who has grief like I do?' he mumbled. Then, louder, 'Who is the one who stops the stars in their tracks with his grief?' Then, louder again, almost shouting, 'Who is the one whose grief freezes the sun itself?' And at full volume, facing them all, the shocked bystanders and the incredulous king and queen, he answered his the question. 'It is I, Hamlet the Dane.'

With a flying leap he too jumped into the grave, almost landing on Laertes. 'The devil take your soul,' shouted the aggrieved brother, and threw himself at his childhood friend. Frantically, they wrestled. Above them circled the helpless frightened officials, bleating and protesting. In the pit the two men shook and rattled each other, searching for a good grip, but each unable to get one. 'Separate them, damn you!' the king roared at his servants. 'Separate them!'

One of the footmen, afraid to touch the prince, but more afraid of the king's wrath, jumped down and pulled the two apart, managing to hold both of the sweating, staring men. Only when they were calmer did the servant allow them to climb out of the grave. Even then, Hamlet, spoiling for a proper fight, could not hold his tongue. From the top of the mound, on all fours, spitting like a cat he snarled at Laertes, 'If I have to do battle with you a thousand times to prove my point, I'll do it.'

The queen, unwisely, asked, 'But to prove what point, my dear Hamlet?'

'That I loved Ophelia! Fifty thousand brothers, with all the love they can summon, would not equal my love for her. Ophelia, Ophelia.'

The king stepped across the corner of the grave to stop the enraged Laertes from springing at Hamlet. 'He is mad, Laertes, you know that. Take no notice of him.'

'Hamlet, you must stop this!' Gertrude begged.

But Hamlet, torn apart by shock and sadness, hardly heard them. 'Show me what you would do for her!' he cried, to Laertes, but almost as if to himself. He sank back onto his haunches. 'Would you weep, fight, fast? Would you tear yourself to pieces? Would you drink vinegar? Would you eat scorpions? I would. Do you come here to whine? To outdo me by jumping into her grave? Do you want to be buried with her? Well, so too I, all of these. And if you tell them to build a hill over the grave you share with her, then I'll tell them to put a million acres of earth on her and me, and then another and then another, until they have built a mountain like the world has never seen before. A mountain that touches the sun.' He shook his head and sobbed: bitter dry sobs.

The onlookers were standing well back, alarmed by his ranting. Many had never seen him like this. 'Please, this is nothing, he is upset,' the queen told them. 'Soon he will calm down. Please.'

Laertes, still blocked by Claudius, went to speak, but the raised finger of his monarch stopped him. Not daring even now to flout his commander-in-chief he stayed silent, trembling with feeling. 'Your time will come,' the king whispered to him. 'Not now. Not now.'

Hamlet turned to leave the awful place. As he went he snarled back at Laertes, 'Not even Hercules could stop a cat miaowing or a dog barking. Believe me, this cat will miaow and this dog will have his day.'

He sprang from the mound and ran away into the mist, into the heart of the cemetery.

TWENTY-NINE

Somehow all who lived or worked at Elsinore knew that the day had come. Everyone in Denmark seemed to know it. The wolves loping through forest grinned harder, bared their teeth wider. Cats uncurled, spat at their owners, ran away to cellars and made nests behind bags of potatoes, yet gave birth to no kittens. The milk of goats curdled, or tasted like vinegar.

Brothers and sisters went away from their parents and fought with quiet ferocity, with intent murderous but mute. In Clennstein a baby vomited and died.

Thunder rolled in from the north and the rain slashed across the sky. The wind blew so cold that nothing could keep it out. None went outside except those who were compelled to do so, and they cursed and complained at the snow and the ice and their skimpy clothing. In the castle the baker slapped his apprentice a dozen times before he had even lit the oven. When the bread refused to rise he threw a knife at the boy and called him a bastard, called his own sister's son a bastard.

The cooks went sullenly about their work, thinking of nothing but sex and hangovers and their hateful jobs. In the chambers and bedrooms the maids shook out blankets and hung clothes, but today everything seemed bespattered and stained. They grimaced as they took sheets away, cringed at the rats creeping through cupboards, moaned with each gust of wind.

Only Garath the gardener sucked on his pipe and said nothing. There were no more strange deaths in his domain these days. No more goslings slung against walls and left to die. No more stabbings under the full moon. Garath was coming to the end of his days, and his secrets would die with him.

Inside the king's favourite conference room the noble majesty of Denmark sat locked together with Laertes. He and Claudius whispered into each other's beards, telling stories of past treasons and present hates.

They stroked as fondly as lovers while they inseminated each other with plots. For a week now they had swapped assurances of malice. Poisoning the air with their foetid breaths and rotten words they gave birth to the plot.

And now it was time.

Hamlet leaned against a corner wall at the west of the parapet, hugging himself with both arms. The wind was democratic: it blew as keenly into his face as into any other's. The snow stung his eyes and melted on his cheeks till it looked like tears. The guards watched him crossly: they were always suspicious that he was there to spy on them. Because of him they had to patrol the walls more assiduously, they had to leave their cold sentry boxes for the colder walls. Because of his brooding presence they had to peer into the driving sleet until their faces blistered. The news of his return would once have filled them with joy, but now it gave them a sense of foreboding. They paid him homage when they saw him but they did their best to linger and stamp their feet at a safe distance along the parapet.

Horatio, however, sought him out, and, as friends do, found him. They hugged joyfully. The wind could find no chink in their friendship. Seeing them locked together, an observer from far off might have thought he was looking at a new species of bear. Both were dressed in green jackets and black pants. Horatio wore a brown scarf and white hat, Hamlet wore a deep red scarf and was bare-headed. Against the grey stone wall they stood out: they were alive.

'Welcome back,' Horatio said, when the hug was done. 'In spite of the circumstances, I welcome you back to Elsinore.'

'Elsinore. Or else I snore. Or else I sleep. I have done too much sleeping, Horatio. We have all done too much of that. I am done with sleeping.'

'Hamlet, a man who does not sleep must die.'

'And a man who dies does nothing but sleep. Away with sleep, I say. If the king had his way I would be asleep now, and a long sleep it would be.'

Horatio stirred, and checked that his collar was high around his neck, keeping out the bitter cold. He was afraid that the prince might again say dangerous words, voice dangerous thoughts.

'Look there at what you see, Horatio.' Hamlet threw his right arm out to embrace the view of the graveyard, the river, Clennstein, the plains and the forest. Fields formed a chessboard with many shades of black, and a white road wound its way down the valley, like a ghostly snake. 'It is worth keeping the eyes open for that.'

'Indeed. It is your home. One day, dei volentes, it will be your kingdom.'

'Do you want to hear what happened to me? Why I am back in Denmark instead of arriving in England?'

'Yes, of course.'

'I acted rashly, Horatio. I felt a rash and I scratched it. And sometimes when we act rudely and quickly, without thinking, it works out for the best. And do you know what that tells me?'

'No.'

'It tells me that an energy carves out our futures for us, and although we take a hammer and chisel and try to reshape them we do so without effect.'

'"There's a divinity that shapes our ends,"' Horatio muttered, '"rough-hew them how we will."'

Hamlet looked at him with surprise and pleasure. 'Yes, that's it! Where did you get that from?'

'I don't know. I read it somewhere.'

'I'd like to get that book.'

He said nothing more for several minutes, until Horatio dared to ask, 'You were saying that you acted rashly, and it worked out for the best?'

'Yes.' Hamlet's tone became matter-of-fact. 'On the boat for England I could not sleep. My heart was in a state of civil war. Something about the two people who accompanied me, and their dealings with my noble stepfather, added to my chaos. In the middle of the night I went to the cabin of Rosencrantz and Guildenstern. I took the letters they carried from Claudius. I went back to my cabin and broke open the seal and read the contents. And what did I find, Horatio?' He gave a nervous laugh. 'Why, a request to have my head struck from my shoulders by his English friends. By the king's friends.'

Horatio stood and took several agitated paces towards the other side of the parapet, away from his prince and friend. 'Hamlet, is such infamy possible?'

Hamlet gazed steadily at him until Horatio realised he was not going to get an answer to his question. He asked, 'What did you do then?'

'I love certainty,' the young prince replied almost without blinking. 'When I am certain of my ground I build what I need and what is right. I wrote a new letter to England, a fine letter, pretending to be from the king, asking a favour: that as England was a friend of Denmark so she would do us a great service by putting the carriers of my letter to death.'

Horatio gulped. This was a resolute prince indeed. This is a man I could follow into battle, he thought. But then, almost as quickly, came a second thought: Why did he have to get the English to do the killing for him? Out loud, he said, 'How did you seal it?'

'I have the seal of my late father. It so resembles that of my uncle that no one would notice the difference.'

'And so,' said Horatio slowly, trying to adjust to a new world without these two young aesthetes, whom he had known all their lives. He remembered his father saying that they would come to no good. It seemed that they were coming to bad, very bad. 'And so, Rosencrantz and Guildenstern go to their deaths.'

'I have no conscience about them. They stepped between two opposing forces, like flies that buzz between the right hand of a man and his left. Now the hands have slapped together.

'Soon the word will come from England that Rosencrantz and Guildenstern have been splattered like flies. The king will know.

'And in the short time before that happens, the space is mine. The earth and the sky and this castle are mine. All I regret, apart from my wasted life, is the way I treated Laertes at the cemetery. I lost my senses there and I am sorry for it. To me, Laertes and I are in the same room, looking at each other in mirrors.'

'His grief is great. He has lost his father and his sister, and he believes that you…'

'Yes, that I am responsible. I who am irresponsible. But he's right enough, on the face of it. I caused the deaths, in the same way that a Danish archer kills a Norwegian foot-soldier, and at that moment neither man thinks of the kings who started the war.'

They walked in silence along the parapet until they came at last to shelter in the officer's post.

'There's someone coming,' Horatio said.

It was Osric. 'Ah, Your Royal Highness, my lord,' he said, pulling off his hat and giving an exaggerated bow to Hamlet, and then Horatio. 'Here you are. Not easy to find. Well, well. I trust you are both well? Highness, what a terrible homecoming, to hear the sad news in such a way. She was a splendid creature, to be sure, the finest looking filly in Elsinore.'

He seemed nervous, prattling like a child in front of a strict and feared teacher.

'You may put your hat back on your head,' Hamlet said. 'It belongs there: that is its right and proper place.'

'Why, thank you my lord. It is a cold day. I am most exceedingly grateful.'

'Now, there you are wrong,' Hamlet said. 'It is actually quite warm with this southerly wind.'

'Warm? Well, yes indeed, there is a warm aspect to the wind. Yes, yes, you are right, sir. I have not been out in it long enough to understand how warm it truly is.'

'Sultry,' Hamlet remarked thoughtfully, gazing around him. A few drops of sleet, almost snow, blew around him. 'Very sultry and hot for my complexion.'

'It is that, sir, why, for your complexion, yes, yes, I can understand that the sun would burn on such a day. Very sultry, very hot, why, that's true.'

He took a confidential step forwards and whisked off his hat again. Hamlet coughed discreetly and nodded at the offending item. Osric blushed and restored it to his head. He had been about to speak but he now had too many issues to deal with. It took him some seconds to remember what he wanted to say.

'The king, his royal majesty,' he began, and was so moved at the thought of his royal master that he reverently removed his hat again, 'has sent me to you...'

'The hat,' Hamlet said.

'Ah, the hat. The hat? Oh yes, I beg Your Royal Highness's pardon. I am a little over-heated.'

'Heat? Would you call today hot?'

'Well, well, perhaps not exactly hot, sir, but tending towards heat at times.'

He wiped his brow. 'The hat,' Hamlet reminded him again.

'Ah!' The hat went back on the head and Osric plunged in again. 'The fact is, noble sir, that the king, his royal majesty, has asked me to step in your direction to speak to you, sir, of Laertes. Now there is nobility, sir, both of you sirs, Laertes is a man who is the very definition of a gentleman. If I were to write a book, and I have sometimes thought that I might or should, if I were to write a book on the make-up of a gentleman, what constitutes a gentleman and so forth, and if I were to write it entirely about Laertes I would not go very far wrong, insofar as his manners, indeed his manner to all people…'

'Well, you do him credit, and he deserves every word you say,' Hamlet said. 'In fact to my mind it is almost disrespectful to Laertes to speak of him with your hat upon your head.'

Osric jumped as though flicked with a wet towel. 'I meant no disrespect I assure you, sir,' he said with an embarrassed giggle. He swept the hat off and bowed flamboyantly, then in a rush said, 'The king has staked six Barbary horses in a bet with Laertes, who has bet six French swords in return. I have been sent here to tell you that.'

'Put on your hat,' said Hamlet in a kindly tone. 'I would not have your ears catch cold.'

Osric did so but now he was getting sulky.

'What kind of swords?' Horatio asked, with the interest of a professional.

Osric doffed his hat again to speak to Horatio. 'I know not exactly, my lord, but I warrant they would be of the finest, and I believe they come with girdles and straps and hangers, all in all, sir, a prize worth winning.'

He turned to Hamlet and made to speak, but just as he took in breath Hamlet mouthed the word 'hat', and Osric collapsed again.

'Well, I assume this bet involves the prince,' Horatio suggested. 'Perhaps you had better tell our royal master how it concerns him.'

Now Osric had his cue and nothing could stop him. He leaned in again, in his confidential way, towards Horatio, whom he felt he could trust. 'They were talking, his royal majesty and Laertes, about swordsmanship, and of course everyone knows the prowess of Laertes, noble and starred youth that he is, but the king would have it that you, sir Hamlet, are not to be sneezed at, and so the bet was made. Laertes is certain you cannot get within three hits of him, and so he offers to fight you seven rounds, saying you will not win more than two. In other words if he beats you by five to two, then the horses are his, but should he only beat you by four to three, then the outcome is the opposite.'

'What if Hamlet should beat Laertes by, say, seven to nothing?' Horatio asked.

Osric smiled indulgently and doffed his hat to the prince. 'The affair would not proceed past the third round in that eventuality, and of course Laertes would lose his rapiers.'

'And what is Laertes' weapon of choice?' asked Hamlet.

'Rapier and dagger.'

'That's two, but let it be.'

'Will Your Royal Highness accept the challenge?' Osric asked eagerly.

Hamlet thought, but only for a moment. 'You may tell the king that I will walk in the great hall in an hour or so. I won't fight with daggers; they are weapons for assassins. But if rapiers are brought and the gentleman likes to attend, then I shall do my best to win the king's bet for him.'

Osric was enraptured. 'How chivalrous!' He held his hat over his heart. 'Truly, you and Laertes are well-matched. Perfect, sir, perfect. I shall inform his royal majesty, if the prince will give me leave to…er… leave.'

'Certainly.'

After Osric exited, with more flourishes and bows, Hamlet turned to Horatio. 'Who knows what this is about? But it is good I think. Something may happen or it may not, but at least there is movement.'

'You had better be careful of Laertes. I believe he improved greatly whilst in France.'

'I've beaten men who have beaten him,' Hamlet said excitedly. 'You don't realise all the practice I've been having. I've been training hard the last year, with some fine teachers. Prince Heinrich von Bellheim for one, and M. Paul D'Eglantine. A start of three? I'll win easily.'

Horatio smiled. He had never heard Hamlet boast before.

'I think I've been approaching this the wrong way,' Hamlet said. 'I've been wanting to design the world all over again, to rearrange it according to… well, according to the way my father would have wanted it. But I haven't been able to, and that's because I'm not God. This is better now. This way I don't create a new world, I just tweak it a little. As it flows along I move a rock or take away a dead branch. I'm not in charge of the world. That was a conceit on my part.'

Horatio nodded. He was not entirely sure what Hamlet was talking about, but that was common enough. He appreciated that at least, since his return, the prince seemed rational with him. He suspected no one else saw that side of Hamlet any more. But this was a new mood now. Hamlet looked absurdly young again. There was a freshness about him, an energy. Something about the bet had excited him. It seemed that the thought of action had tipped him into a new state. 'The thought of action', there was a funny idea. Didn't they contradict each other, those words, 'thought' and 'action'?

Horatio smiled to himself. He opened his mouth but it was Osric who spoke. The foolish young man had returned to the rocky point where they were sheltering from the bitter wind, and was standing in front of them. He held his hat behind his back and spoke with less ceremony. 'Your Royal Highness, his majesty sends me to ask if your pleasure is still to play with Laertes, and whether you will do so now, or whether you need a longer time?'

Hamlet shrugged but Horatio could sense that he was bursting. 'I am as always the king's to command. If he is in a rush, I will accommodate him.'

Rather more confidently, Osric performed a bow, and replaced his hat on his head. 'Sir, the king and the queen and indeed all the court are on their way to the hall now to enjoy the entertainment.'

'Then I too am nearly at the entrance. Not here, Osric, but just outside the hall. Half a dozen steps away.'

Horatio expected that this would be enough for Osric, but not so. Now he executed another bow, removed his hat and added, 'Most Excellent Highness, I am bidden by that most noble lady the queen your mother to convey a further request to you.'

Hamlet was leaning against the stone wall, as he had been for some time. Yet Horatio was aware that he was never still. Now, at Osric's words, Hamlet stood rigidly, and the difference was stark. The twitching finger, the lively eyes, the nervous jiggle, all were gone as he waited in straining silence to hear the message from his mother. What power she has over him, Horatio thought.

Hamlet waited until Osric spoke again.

'Well, noble prince, it is simply this, that she desires you speak warmly to Laertes before the bouts begin. I believe she seeks a rapprochement. I understand there was a certain indelicacy at the cemetery…I was not able to attend, but the queen spoke most feelingly upon her return…'

Hamlet seemed to shudder for a moment. Horatio could not understand his reaction. But he sounded willing enough when he answered. 'She gives good advice.'

Osric made off, glad to be gone. Hamlet drummed his bottom lip with a finger. Horatio waited to hear what he would say. At last he spoke. 'He thinks he is the new Polonius,' he remarked.

'Osric?'

'Yes. Pulling our strings and expecting us to dance. But Osric to Polonius is as a stuffed sheep to a fox.' Horatio didn't reply. After a minute Hamlet added, 'You wouldn't believe how sick at heart I feel, Horatio. A strangeness has come over me.'

'Sir,' Horatio began.

But Hamlet cut him off. 'It's nothing. It might

trouble a woman perhaps, but I'm not letting it concern me.'

Horatio took a step towards him. 'Hamlet,' he said, 'if your heart dislikes anything, obey it. Trust your instincts, which are good ones. I'll go and tell them you're not fit and they'll have to postpone.'

'No, no. I defy these feelings. When a sparrow falls from the sky, it affects the whole universe. If something happens now, it won't happen later; if it happens later, it won't happen now. Since no one leaves with anything, what does it matter when we leave?'

Again Horatio was baffled by his friend. He stared at him as the sky turned red around them and the new detachment of guards marched past to take over the watch.

THIRTY-ONE

The great hall was the coldest place in Elsinore. Even with huge logs banked in the giant fireplaces at either end the temperature seemed hardly above freezing. The king sprawled on his cedar throne, crown by his side, a pewter mug to hand. Despite the temperature, he was hot and sweaty and from time to time wiped his brow with a grimy handkerchief.

The queen, in white fur robes, sat on a settee, avoiding the throne beside her husband. She too seemed nervous. Horatio wondered if she had lost weight; she looked much leaner, almost gaunt. He remembered how when he was little she had seemed kind, most of the time, remembering to order Horatio's favourite meals after his mother died, giving him little presents for his birthday, taking the boys to the circus. She had never been warm or funny or loving, the way Horatio's own mother had been, but he had never felt unwelcome at the palace. He knew she could be sarcastic, and that she could lose her temper in an instant, but when she was in a bad mood he and Hamlet had learned to melt away to the tower or the woods or the fields, and let the servants suffer her wrath.

The sudden passing of the old king, Hamlet's father, had put Denmark on a different path, but no one had been sure at first where it would lead. There had been trepidation, and almost a stench around the new regime from the first days, but as far as Horatio knew, these feelings had not been articulated by anyone. Gertrude had still been all right, he thought. A bit grimmer, a bit sharper, a bit more cynical. Just a bit more of everything really.

The most noticeable changes had come since the death of Polonius. Nothing had gone right for her and her new husband these last few months. It was as though the old man's death had put an end to the momentum of the tawdry couple. Hamlet's mad stabbing of Polonius had been like a kiss of corruption on the lips of the royal couple. It had blocked all exits, closed off all possibilities.

Hamlet and Horatio walked into the great hall as though they were actors entering a scene. All the others were assembled, not just the king and queen, but Laertes, standing alone and carving figures in the air with a rapier, Osric, dancing in front of the throne like an annoying grasshopper, three ladies to wait upon the queen, a group of minor lords clustered around the king, attendants and servants and courtiers, spectators and minor relatives...The two young men stood out. Hamlet for his sheer physical beauty, of course, but those in the castle were used to that. It was more that he and Horatio possessed a certain lightness of being. It would not be too fanciful to say that a glow surrounded them. They seemed as much like acrobats as actors, connected to the earth only by the thinnest of lines, almost invisible bonds.

The great hall fell still as they entered. Horatio came to a halt halfway between the door and the thrones. Hamlet went forward alone. The only person moving in the whole vast space, he was the focus of every eye. He strode straight up to Laertes. 'If I have hurt you, Laertes,' he said in a strong voice, 'I say now, in the company of all present, that I regret it. I have not been myself. And if I am not myself, then whoever wronged you was not me. In fact, the unbalanced Hamlet who wronged you wronged me also, for to be out of my own mind is not a condition I would ever desire.'

Laertes swallowed. He had been caught off-guard. 'Your Royal Highness, I accept what you say on a personal level,' he said at last. 'But I cannot yet accept your apology. I must be guided by advisors who are older and wiser. In the meantime, I will treat the friendship you are now demonstrating as though it is true.'

Hamlet had to be satisfied with that. He nodded and turned to take the foil offered to him, while Laertes accepted his from another servant. They each tested the blade.

'Too heavy,' cried Laertes, laying his down.

'I am content,' said Hamlet.

The king watched anxiously. 'You know the wager, Hamlet?' he asked, his voice thick. He had to clear his throat before he spoke, and again as he finished.

'Certainly. But Your Majesty has laid the odds on the weaker side.'

'Well, well, Laertes has made himself a proficient swordsman. But the odds are fair, I think.'

Laertes had chosen his weapon and now turned to face the young prince. The king spoke out again. 'Set the stoups of wine upon that table. If Hamlet scores a hit in the first three rounds I'll drink his health; nay, I'll do more than that. I'll drop a jewel into his glass to spur him further. A jewel brighter than any worn by the last four kings of Denmark! There's motivation for you, my son.'

Claudius burst into a fit of coughing so severe that the two sportsmen waited for him to finish before they began their duel. At last, however, the king was able to signal to them to start. 'Let the judge bear a wary eye,' he commanded, before putting the mug to his lips once more for another long drink.

And so they went to it. Hard, too. The audience knew straight away that this was a match charged with potency for them both. Spectators retreated as the two young men, quick and graceful, slashed at each other from one end of the hall to the other. The beginning was all Laertes; he believed he had improved so much since Hamlet had last seen him that he could take the prince by surprise and score easy points.

Yet smugness allows no other point of view; smugness lacks imagination. It never entered Laertes' head that the prince, who had been his superior when they were children, might have improved too. In truth, Hamlet had spent as many hours at practice as Laertes, and with better teachers.

At first Hamlet foxed, doing no more than he had to, allowing Laertes to believe that victory would be quick. But Laertes found attack after attack failing, finding space where there should have been flesh, or Hamlet's rapier where there should have been an opening, and he began to suspect that this might not go as easily as he had planned. And then, in the course of a spectacular turn which should have left Hamlet's flank exposed, Laertes heard his opponent cry out, 'A hit!'

'No,' shouted Laertes, but wondering if there might have been a sting on his right side.

'Judgment!' demanded Hamlet, with staring eyes.

'A hit, a palpable hit,' confirmed the judge.

In his excitement the king rose from his throne. He seemed more than excited, agitated even. Horatio thought he was drunk.

'Again! Let's go again,' shouted Laertes, who was flushed and angry, suspecting that he had been betrayed by his own sense of superiority.

'Wait,' croaked Claudius. 'Wait, the pair of you. I promised Hamlet he should have a jewel should he score a strike, and a jewel he shall have.'

Hamlet scowled at his stepfather but the man appeared not to notice. With some difficulty, fumbling in his robes, Claudius found a large diamond and held it up to the light. The courtiers gasped, and a lady-in-waiting squealed. Osric broke into excited applause. 'Most generous, Your Majesty,' he shouted. 'Exceedingly generous.'

The king gazed proudly around the great hall. 'This is the way we govern,' he proclaimed. 'There is plenty for everyone.' He nodded to a servant and the man, trembling with cold in his threadbare uniform, hurried to fetch Hamlet's glass of wine. The king held it aloft and, after a last glance at the crowd, dropped the diamond into it. People gasped again, giggled, then a soft tide of whispers ran everywhere at once, like foam fizzing on the beach. Claudius dropped back onto his throne, wiping his face again and nodding to the same servant to refill his glass.

'I fancy that was rather well done, my dear,' he said to his wife, in what he imagined to be a whisper, but which was heard all around the hall. She gave only a nod of acknowledgment. Claudius raised his voice again. 'Give Hamlet the glass.'

'Later, later,' Hamlet shouted back. 'After the next round perhaps.'

He did not see the king's glare. Laertes had already launched himself at the prince, hoping to gain the advantage of surprise. It was within the rules but only barely within the conventions of sportsmanship. Hamlet was able to deflect the blade by nothing more than a centimetre, at the same time trying to sway out of the path of its vicious point. Somehow it was enough and the thing passed him by. He twisted away and ran half the length of the hall before ducking to the right, turning, and preparing to face the oncoming Laertes.

Now Laertes fought with cold determination. It was all Laertes, wave after wave of skilful flourishes, at times moving so fast that the crowd could barely see the blade, darting and feinting and stabbing, driving the young prince back and back and back, like a dozen waves breaking in quick succession upon rocks that seemed too weak to withstand them.

Laertes' body and blade had become one, the young man was nothing but movement. Although his mind was diseased, his body, for a brief interval, threw off its knowledge of his intentions and reached the apogee of its physical perfection. Perhaps too the body knew it had only minutes left to live, knew it would soon lie pierced and dying on the floor; perhaps some knowledge of that gave it the power and skill for this last expression of beauty and training.

Whatever, it was a new and glorious Laertes who with passion and grace fought Hamlet. His swordsmanship stopped the breathing of the spectators, returned sudden sobriety to the king, and set the queen swooning on the sofa where she sat.

Then it was over.

THIRTY-TWO

Laertes leapt, twisted and stabbed at the space where Hamlet should have been. For a moment he seemed suspended in the cold air, a god who cared nothing for gravity. But the prince was too quick, and an instant later Laertes felt truth touch him in the side of his ribs.

'Another hit,' shouted Hamlet, emerging from under his opponent like a rat from a collapsed tower.

'A touch, a touch, I do confess,' gasped Laertes. He stood, breathing like man who is about to go to a very different place, one he has never visited before and cannot know. Yet his intention was to send Hamlet there, today, as soon as possible, by means foul or fair.

'Our son shall win,' said the king nervously.

'He's short of breath,' said the queen. 'Look how he sweats. Hamlet, my darling, come.' She went to him, and dabbed at his brows with her napkin, then gave it to him so that he could wipe his whole face. At this cameo, Laertes stared and glared. No one was left now in his family to perform this service for him.

Gertrude turned and saw what she was looking for. A glass of wine. It was Hamlet's. It stood on a small black wooden table, cold and alone. She picked it up. The king thought she was about to offer it to Hamlet and he felt a glow of relief. If it came from her hand the prince would surely drink! Claudius was so close to the solution! Why the young man was here at all instead of lying in two parts in an English graveyard was a mystery for which he had no explanation, but no matter, a sip from the deadly mixture would clear the air of Elsinore. Drink, drink, drink it!

Instead the queen raised the glass to her lips. 'A toast to your good fortune, Hamlet,' she said, in her thick, luscious voice.

Claudius felt paralysis numbing his feet at the same time as it froze his heart. Nevertheless he managed to half rise from the throne. 'Dear Gertrude,' he croaked.

She did not hear him.

He saw the arch of her neck as she exposed it to him for the last time. Her beautiful neck, still smooth and unmarked, after all these years. The glass was at her lips. 'Gertrude,' he shouted. It was as though he had shocked her into drinking. He saw the movement of her throat as the foul wine ran down into her stomach to begin its work. She drank enough. More than enough. A sip would have done.

'Yes?' she asked, putting the glass back on the table and turning towards him.

'Your Majesty, are you all right?' Osric pressed forwards.

The king sank back onto his throne. No matter now. Too late, too late.

'Nothing,' he muttered. 'It is nothing. It is all nothing.' Claudius shuddered and wiped his handkerchief over his face. In the space of a moment everything had gone irreversibly wrong. His reign was over; his life would probably be forfeit. After all, the ancient curse was on him. He had killed his own brother. In his bowels he had always expected this.

Gertrude shrugged. Her hand still held the cup. She offered it now to the prince. Claudius watched, indifferent. Hamlet would drink or he would not. He would live or he would not. It didn't seem important any more. Through the window at the end of the hall the king saw three swans on the mound above the pond. The shadows of the castle made them look black. He almost smiled. Black swans. The day swans turned black, truly that would be the end of the world.

'I dare not drink yet, madam. In a while.' Hamlet pushed his mother away.

'Come, let me wipe your face properly.' Her voice was more throaty than ever. There had been a time when Claudius had thrilled to that voice. All through those years while his brother courted and won her and took her, the younger man had been a willing prisoner of her voice. Now Claudius had her, and he thought her voice sounded like the honk of a swan.

She clung to Hamlet, but he tried to push her away again. Claudius became aware that Laertes had somehow drifted to a position near the throne. With everyone watching the mother and son, the young man muttered, 'Your Majesty, I could do it now. I'll hit him now.'

Both of them knew of the deadly venom on Laertes' sword. They knew because they had anointed the tip themselves, not much more than half an hour earlier. None but they knew. They were a pretty pair, these two, one intent on power, one on revenge, and both riddled through and through with the most potent force of all, hatred.

'No, no,' the king mumbled. 'Not now.'

'This is not the time to be troubled by conscience,' Laertes whispered, as if to himself. 'Even so I am troubled…'

But no one heard him say it, so perhaps he did not say it.

They all heard a scornful Hamlet. He had cast his mother away. She staggered, although he had used no force. Now he challenged Laertes. 'Come for the third round, Laertes. You are wasting our time. Don't you take me seriously? Or are you getting nervous?'

'Say you so?' bellowed Laertes. 'Come on then.'

He rushed out in a clumsy charge more fitted to a drunk farmer trying to drive a cow into a bail. Hamlet was disconcerted and missed an easy chance for a hit. For a few moments the young men, so graceful and accomplished in the previous round, fought with all the skill of five year olds wrestling in a sandpit. They met and grappled and parted again, three times, except that as they parted from the third grappling both stabbed at each other. They turned to the judge, each hoping he might have nicked the other.

There was a pause then the judge, an old man named Voltimand, said quietly, 'Nothing either way.'

Hamlet grimaced and made to step back, to ready himself for the resumption. As he did, Laertes, now chaotic with rage, shouted, 'Have at you now,' and with a sudden awful stab wounded Hamlet in the arm.

He felt a certain dark relief, that the poison was now irreversibly inside the prince's body. Ophelia could rest in whatever peace she was able to attain, and his father could go to his last destination. But he was unprepared for the immediate outcome. With a roar Hamlet threw himself upon the young man, he who had once been his friend and who, unbeknownst still to Hamlet, had now murdered him.

The two fought furiously and had to be dragged from each other. Hamlet felt a curious buzzing in the head but was not yet slowed by the poison. The moment they were released both rushed for their rapiers and picked them up.

'You've got the wrong ones,' called Osric, but neither man took notice. Hamlet heard the words but attached no importance to them. Either sword suited him well enough. Laertes heard the words but did not understand them until a sudden tearing pain burned into his heart. It all happened so quickly. The cut on his chest was nothing yet it was everything. The pain should have been slight but it was the bearer of a deeper pain that could not be borne. Laertes dropped to one knee, realising with awfulness what had happened and now hearing Osric's words properly. 'The wrong sword,' he whispered. 'The wrong sword.'

Osric appeared at his side. 'My lord, are you all right?'

'All right? No Osric, all wrong.'

As if through a dense thundercloud he heard someone call, 'Look after the queen, quick, something's wrong.'

'She's fainted.'

'Get a doctor.'

Laertes looked up and saw Horatio at Hamlet's side. To his right he saw the queen lying on the floor, surrounded by attendants. He heard Hamlet asking, 'The queen? My mother? What is wrong with her?'

From the throne came the king's frightened voice. He seemed unable to move. 'She swoons to see her son bleed.'

'My lord, are you all right?' Osric asked again. 'What is it? Are you hurt?'

Before Laertes could answer, the queen's voice, suddenly shrill with fear, cried, 'No, no, the drink, oh God, the drink, it was poisoned. Dear Hamlet, I am poisoned.'

Despair filled Laertes. His voice filled the hall, even though he did not seem to speak any louder than usual. 'Like a rabbit caught in his own trap, Osric, I am killed with my own treachery.' He forced himself to stand. When he did he found himself confronting Hamlet again.

The prince was struggling to his feet, his face demented. 'Let the doors be locked!' Hamlet shouted. 'There is villainy here. There is treachery. I will seek it out.'

Laertes felt an extraordinary calm. A new strength entered him, to sustain him for the last moments of his life. 'You do not have to seek far, Hamlet,' he said. 'It is here, in me. Hamlet, you are murdered. You have only a few minutes to live. The weapon is in your own hands: the sword you hold is poisoned. It is I who applied the poison to it, and it is fitting that the foul wasp has turned on me and stung me as well. Your mother has sipped poisoned wine, which we also meant for you.'

With no warning, all his strength rushed from him. He was staggered by its swiftness. He dropped to his knees. No act in his life took more resolve than the simple raising of his hand to point at the king. 'There is your enemy,' he said. With a sudden surge, a last expression of the life force, he stood, then in an instant fell forwards, lifeless, hitting the hard stone floor with a thud that must have broken every bone in his face.

To see Horatio now was to see love at work. His expression was as demented as Hamlet's but he held his friend even as he shouted to the servants to carry out his prince's orders. 'Seal the doors! Let no one leave. Let no one draw a weapon, should he set any value on his life. Hamlet, over here.'

He tried to draw Hamlet to a seat but the prince threw him off easily and staggered to his mother. He had so much he wanted to explain to her. He wanted to tell her all the reasons he had, for everything he had ever done, everything. But time had lost interest in them both. Time had already turned itself to other affairs. Gertrude had slipped away while the men were shouting, her tortured soul gone to another world where her first husband awaited her and her second was about to join her. Her eyes were closed and her skin cooling. The ladies-in-waiting were starting to step back, to distance themselves. Gertrude had never inspired affection or devotion in other women and they understood already that their futures lay elsewhere. They had to think of themselves.

Hamlet wanted to shout obscenities at them for their lack of loyalty—they did not love his mother as much as he did, and that was unforgivable—but he knew time would not spare him for such things. All he could hope now was that it would grant him another minute, for the last task of his life, the one he had been charged to do so long ago. His failure to execute it had caused chaos. It had caused tragedy.

Claudius trembled to see him coming. 'Guards,' he called feebly. 'Guards, seize him.'

'Let no one move!' bellowed Horatio. He held a rapier in each hand. Feet apart, he faced the guards. 'Move, and I'll skewer you.'

No one moved and Claudius watched the terrible spectre come at him. Hamlet's face appeared to be all stubble and eyes, not grey any more, but white, with no discernible pupils. He was relentless. A rapier appeared as if by magic in his hand and Claudius found enough spirit to stand. The sword ran him through. A cold line went through him from front to back and the king understood that nothing would ever be the same again. The line ignited and turned to fire inside him, an awful fire that burned everywhere and could not be put out. 'Guards,' he whispered, 'guards, I am not yet dead. I might yet live. Put a stop to this. Stop him.'

No one responded.

'Not yet dead?' the ghastly apparition screeched at him. 'Then try this.' The prince's hand was at his face; the back of the hand hit him and it hurt; how it hurt; didn't the prince realise he was hurting him? He should stop. Claudius's mouth was forced open and cold wine was splashing inside him. Perhaps it could put out the fire. Perhaps this was love. The king drank eagerly. Yes, it was working, the fire was going out, the furnace in his stomach was becoming cold. The wine turned into a snake and crawled down into its hole and wrapped itself around the hot bear that now lived in his bowels it was a desert and ice rolled across it and all turned to ice it became a cave the blackest cave Claudius had ever been in too black nothing could be this black or this cold and the king's eyes rolled back in his head and he died.

But by then Hamlet was lying on the floor, his head cradled in Horatio's lap, his face beginning to contort as death went to work on him. 'May heaven take care of Laertes,' he said. 'I will follow him soon enough. Oh, Horatio, I feel I have everything to say, and I know there is no time to say any of it. At least be sure to tell the world what you know. Tell my story fully and frankly, but try to find some virtue in me when you do.'

A spasm shook him; he clenched his eyes and teeth, but soon it passed. He hardly seemed to hear Horatio's staunch statement: 'I will follow you, beloved friend, there is wine in the glass yet.'

But when Horatio reached for the fatal dregs Hamlet pushed his arm away.

'Give me the cup,' he begged. 'Do not take that easy path. Stay in the world instead, and speak for me. I fear the reputation I will leave.' He half sat up, racked by pain. 'Horatio, I beg of you, forget your own pain a while and defend my good name.'

Horatio marvelled that the bright and beautiful prince had come to this, caught up so intensely in his fear for the regard of history. But no sooner had the thought crept into his brain than Hamlet lay down again, whispering, 'I suppose I am King of Denmark for these few brief moments. Let the crown pass to Fortinbras, Horatio.' He raised his voice and shouted through the great hall, 'I am Hamlet, King of the Danes and I say the crown shall pass to Fortinbras.'

'Your Majesty,' Horatio murmured to him. 'It shall be as you say. Fortinbras.'

Hamlet coughed and cramped and coughed again, then whispered to Horatio, 'The rest is silence.'

Horatio held him for some minutes more. He could not tell when life left his friend. In time Voltimand tapped him kindly on the shoulder. 'My lord,' said the older man, 'we have much to do. Our duties lie elsewhere now. It is over. We must prepare the kingdom for the news, send urgent messages to Fortinbras, and begin the funeral rites. My lord, come away.'

Horatio sat there another long minute. A servant handed him a cushion and he placed it under Hamlet's head. He climbed awkwardly to his feet. He looked down at his friend's body. 'Goodnight, sweet prince,' he said. 'May flights of angels sing you to your rest.'

		CANCELLED	

QLD. LIBRARY SUPPLIES